Snowball Earth

Andrea Lisowski
Max Fink

For everyone who deserves better, for everyone who made it this far, and for gals with or without pals.

We would like to thank HK, Valentine, Cronin, Ski, and TJ for all of their wonderful support.

CHAPTER ONE

STAR CLUB MAGAZINE, SEPTEMBER 2015, $6.99
TANYA RAYNE AND JOAN DEVINITA BATTLE ON STAGE AND OFF

JOAN DEVINTIA SHUNS FORMER MENTOR
"Our working relationship is ancient history…
Some things are just better left in the past – like
her music." –J.D.
"Joan is no f*cking saint." –T.R.

"That is such fucking bullshit. I never fucking said that!"

Running her fingers over the soft, blonde fuzz of her shaved head, Joan huffed and shoved the offensive literature away. The gossip magazine slid across the restaurant table and almost tipped over one of her empty glasses. Joan didn't know what she was doing reading that five-dollar piece of trash. Everyone in the business told her to stay away from it – like the front-runner of Despite Darkness, Tanya, who had done nothing but treat Joan with kindness and respect. There was no feud, never had been.

Joan opened for Tanya's band on last year's around-the-country tour. Being on the same stage as the rock goddess was the best kind of ego boost. If there was any animosity for the paparazzi to feed on, it was when the two argued about where to eat next on the road.

The music industry wasn't far enough removed from Hollywood. The masses needed their rumors, and the magazines needed their pushy photographers. Joan couldn't be too hard on the public and the platform that brought her into stardom. She was a rocker, first and foremost. Thanks to an amazing manager who let her stay in one of his penthouse properties rent free, she could spend what money she had from an infant career on dinner at her favorite Thai restaurant. But The Orchid was about to close and the friend who jokingly gave her the magazine had already gone home.

After paying her bill, she folded the magazine and placed it into her shoulder bag. Among lipsticks and a phone charger, was an old baseball cap and a case with Ray-Ban aviators. Joan told herself she didn't need either of them to disguise herself tonight. She wasn't that well-known, and San Diego didn't have that big of a paparazzi scene. Anxiety still worked its way between her ribs and raised her heartbeat as she pushed open the etched-glass doors.

The city was busy tonight. On the sidewalk, she was just another young soul going to a good time or leaving one. With a deep breath of warm, dry air, Joan drew a hand through her hair, moving pale locks away from her undercut. She placed her other hand around the strap of her purse and scanned the area for trouble. As wonderful and relaxed as San Diego was, there was no such thing as a city safe for women.

Several blocks later, goosebumps rose on the back of her neck. It shouldn't be possible to *feel* someone's gaze, but she did. She glanced over her shoulder, blue eyes flashing in the direction that unsettled her most. Behind her, there was a couple taking selfies in front of a tree strung up in white lights. A taxi stopped beside her and let out a man who was destined for the liquor store on the other side

2

of the road. She didn't see anything or anyone interested in her, but she picked up the pace anyway.

Designer boots eating pavement, Joan turned her head forward just in time to stop herself from colliding with a solid figure.

"Hello, Joan."

The bowl of tom kha gai turned over in the blonde's stomach at the sight of a man in a red tie. Instinct took over, forcing her to look for an out instead of at *him*. She ran for the taxi, letting herself in and banging the door shut.

"The Marmax Hotel," she said, slamming her palm down on the door lock.

The cabbie pursed his lips at the rough treatment of his vehicle. "Be gentle," he ordered. "It's a lease."

Looking outside, Joan muttered an apology. The cab pulled away from an empty sidewalk. The man was nowhere to be found.

Joan Devintia was a fighter; she was a take-no-shit-but-give-plenty-back, beer-drinking, guitar-smashing, blonde bitch. But for the last few weeks, VH1's rumored to be Newcomer of the Year had acquired herself a stalker. She didn't know about him at first. That despondent, forgettable face in the concert crowds became familiar as she noticed it more and more often. And then she began to see him elsewhere, always wearing the same bright red tie and an expensive-looking business suit. He was at clubs, restaurants, her manager's house… Stan the Stalker, she called him. A nickname made the situation easier to dismiss, but she couldn't lie to herself anymore.

This was getting ridiculous. She was in the middle of recording a CD, and until *Snowball Earth* came out, she was tethered to San Diego and her studio. If she didn't feel safe enough to go out, she was going to have to do what her manager suggested

3

some time ago. Joan needed to get herself a bodyguard.

~*~

Carmen Savedra went straight from high school into the military. When most of her classmates were talking to college advisors, she was being courted by recruiters. Despite a locker full of Air Force pencils, Army notebooks, and a Navy T-shirt – she chose the Marines. Two weeks after graduation, she left for boot camp. From Small Town, Ohio, Carmen moved on to greatness.

Her transformation into a Marine was a point of pride. After basic and specialized training, she got the eagle, globe, and anchor sigil tattooed to her shoulder. Four years and many countries later, her ink and her love for the military faded.

Now, she was in the last year and a half of her inactive duty. The Marine Corps required a minimum of four years of active duty, followed by another four of inactive duty. People were allowed to return to civilian life during that time, but they were subject to being reactivated if the country went back to war and their service was needed.

As with so many others, she struggled to find decent employment back in the 'real world.' Everyone always assumed that military service would translate to good qualifications for employment, but that was hardly the case. Only officers seemed to get the proper recommendations, and they tended to make the military their career.

After the hundredth disappointment, Carmen decided it was time for a change. She moved from Ohio to California, where she knew she could find a decent, steady paycheck doing what she did best. She bounced back and forth from Los Angeles, to San

4

Diego, to Silicon Valley after she got her private officer license. People hired her for protection services, whether it was a short-term engagement for a single event or someone who needed more attention, she was happy to have a paying job.

Of course, the job was in a male-dominated field. She'd dealt with that in the Corps, so it wasn't a big change. She had an advantage to her male counterparts, though. Not everyone was comfortable with a seven-foot-tall beast following them around everywhere. Carmen was a little more discrete but just as effective.

Many of the management agencies in California had her information, which kept her steadily employed for the most part. The celebrity lifestyle was very public and bright, so breaks between jobs were welcome.

Less than 36 hours after her last assignment ended, Carmen woke up to the noise of her phone ringing and vibrating. Grumbling, she reached across her bed and grabbed the device. With the clumsy swipe of a finger, her quiet time was over.

"This better be good," she said groggily, rolling onto her back once more.

"Is this Carmen Savedra?" a male voice questioned.

"Depends on who wants to know."

"My name is Jerry Stevenson. I am Joan Devintia's agent. I have your information as a private officer on file. You've done some gigs for me before," the man explained. "I'd like to hire you again for Ms. Devintia."

"At... two in the morning?" Carmen questioned.

"That just shows you how serious of a situation Ms. Devintia is in," the agent reasoned. "As soon as you're able to start, I'd like to hire you."

The Latina thought it over, briefly considering turning down the offer just because she was disturbed in the middle of a dreamless sleep. But, it wouldn't be wise to turn down work – word could spread and she'd find herself without a paycheck again.

"Text me the address of your office. I'll be there by nine," she said before hanging up.

She tossed the phone away so it would be harder to hear when the text came across. Pulling a pillow further up under her head, she settled in and huffed. She would be at the office on time, just as she said, but right now she was praying for a dark, dead to the world kind of rest.

CHAPTER TWO

Joan took a cab from her penthouse to Jerry's office. Holding a latte in one hand and her music notes from last night in the other, she pushed open the front door to her manager's office with her shoulder. Her phone buzzed inside her jacket; it was Jerry calling her for the umpteenth time that morning. She was running an hour late.

"I'm coming! Jesus!" Joan cursed his lack of patience. Jerry was an exceptional, white-collar manager. He handled everything from booking gigs, securing a respectable record label, promoting the music – to managing Joan's social media presence, and hiring someone to refine the rock star's wardrobe and look. She was lucky to have him; that didn't mean he was as lucky to have her.

Jerry, an older man with a bald spot on his head that got bigger every time Joan was late, placed his cell phone on his desk and frowned. "Morning, Joan. I was starting to think I wasted Ms. Savedra's time today."

Joan rolled her eyes, using the paltry move to turn her gaze from Jerry's unamused face to a serious one across the room. She got a good look at Ms. Savedra, noticing that she was taller than her new bodyguard by a handful of inches. But, after subtracting the height of her heels, she realized she would only come out a couple inches ahead. The woman was definitely more fit than her and of Hispanic descent. Dark hair cascaded around the Latina's shoulders, and her brown eyes had a certain intensity about them. For her own reasons, Joan had specifically requested a woman for the job.

"*Professionals* are on time and polite," Jerry

tersely reminded his star. With a muted sigh, Joan tossed her notes in a nearby chair so she could free up a hand and greet the newcomer as the fatherly-figure went on. "What are the three P's of a good career?" Jerry was clearly just going to answer his own question anyway, so Joan let him. "Professional, Public, and Private. Act accordingly to the situation."

"Is the situation going to include much more of this?" Joan waved at the tense atmosphere in the room. "Because I have a tune in my head, but I won't for much longer if you keep droning on." She wasn't usually so disagreeable to Jerry's suggestions, but last night had been rough.

Carmen listened to the exchange between musician and manager, having to make an effort not to scowl. She had another P for Jerry: Patronizing. But, she knew the man was good at his job – he'd launched many successful careers. If punctuality was something she was going to need to enforce, then her paycheck just grew by 20%. She was here to keep Joan safe, not babysit her and keep her on schedule.

"So, I hear you're having a bit of a stalker problem," Carmen finally addresses the musician. "Anything you can tell me about what he looks like? Are there any specific places or times he shows up?"

Joan ignored the questions for the moment and held out her hand for the other woman to take. She appreciated that Carmen was being professional, but Joan wasn't interested in talking about her stalker problem right now. It was hard enough calling Jerry in the middle of the night and telling him some of the things that had been going on lately. She wanted to be able to take care of herself in this world. There was something about the spotlight that made her feel invincible. When she wasn't inside that hot light she was vulnerable, and that's what Carmen was here for.

8

Carmen shook with a hard iron grip that was gone before Joan could really register that they were shaking hands.

"He's just... some poser. I don't know," Joan brushed the interview off. There was a studio microphone with her name on it. Not literally of course, but she heard a lot of rappers did that. Joan was more about her music than her name.

That wasn't the answer Carmen wanted. "All right, then... Tell me about your usual schedule," she bid Joan. The sooner that the singer cooperated, the sooner she would be able to go about her usual business.

Joan turned toward her manager, blonde hair flipping over her shoulder as she did so. "Jesus, Jerry. Did you hire a Private Investigator or a bodyguard?" Joan looked back at Carmen. "Body-" She pointed to herself, finger hitting her sternum. "Guard," she ordered.

Carmen quirked a brow. She stepped up to Joan, invading her personal space with an imposing demeanor crafted from years in the service.

"You're the one with the stalker, not me. You're the one who can't walk down the street without everyone and their brother stopping to gawk. And you know what? I don't do attitude. You can find yourself someone else to do the job, princess."

Without another word, she turned and headed for the exit.

Joan shrugged at her manager as Carmen began to walk away. The office door had just shut when Jerry gave her a disappointed look.

"Professionalism," he reminded her before sitting back at his desk and ignoring the problem, as well as Joan.

"Damn it," Joan whispered before rushing after Carmen. She had known Jerry long enough to know his silence could only be interpreted as one thing. Joan had messed up, and he wasn't going to fix it for her. He'd already told her how hard it would be to find a female bodyguard; better to try and repair the infant relationship with Carmen than locate someone else.

Joan practically sprinted out into the parking garage, looking for a sign of the other woman. She spotted Carmen halfway across the lot and jogged to catch up with her. For a short-legged thing, Carmen sure did move fast.

"Ms. Savedra! Please, come back," Joan asked, absent the bitchy attitude she was burdened with earlier. Professional, she reminded herself. "I'm sorry." If she couldn't convince the woman to keep the job, it could be days before Jerry got someone else. The days weren't hard but the evenings were hell. Stan was a bit of a night owl.

At first, Carmen didn't stop. Her black SUV was in sight and she'd dealt with enough primadonnas for one lifetime. If Joan didn't want to take her situation seriously, that was fine. Carmen wasn't going to tag along for the ride. There were plenty of large, bristly guys that would simply stand around to deter people from approaching a singer. But then Joan apologized again.

"I'm sorry, Ms. Savedra. It's just- I'm just scared."

Carmen turned around on a dime, a pointed look on her face. Fear was a great motivator, one of the greatest. The Marine took a steadying breath, inhaling the stench of warm pavement, rubber, and gasoline. She glanced at the car parked next to her. The hatch to its gas tank was open and the cap was missing.

"No more attitude," she ordered.

Not many people talked to Joan like that anymore; she almost missed it – being normal. Almost. Joan nodded and tried to stay polite.

"Yeah. All right." Joan looked over Carmen's shoulder, wondering which car had been Carmen's destination. Her eyes skirted over a few vehicles before she realized she wasn't just looking at the cars. "Can we please go back inside?"

Carmen narrowed her gaze at Joan. "Yeah," she answered quietly. "Lead the way." With marginal observation she could tell the singer was uptight. The way her stare darted around the parking garage – she was looking for someone.

Joan guided them back through the lot. Carmen kept up with her longer strides, just as Joan expected her to. There was something about Carmen that Joan couldn't place. The bodyguard demanded respect and carried herself well.

"If it's okay with you, Ms. Savedra, I normally go to the studio right about now. It's below Jerry's office," she explained as they walked inside the glass building, "in the basement." Jerry was working on assembling a band for her as they were one good drummer short of a full crew. The guys were probably goofing off or just recording various things as they pleased while they waited for Joan to show up.

"That's fine," the other woman responded. "And call me Carmen. Hopefully your schedule won't need to change too much while we're working together." She would allow the singer to do her thing in the studio, but after that they were going to sit down and talk about what she needed to know. "You can consider this the first step toward getting your life back to normal... or as normal as a celebrity's life can be," she added after a moment.

Joan was already rethinking this whole bodyguard idea. Carmen was making it sound like she had gotten herself a babysitter, not a protector. Joan didn't comment on what Carmen said as they took the stairs to the basement. Joan was a bit claustrophobic, and she did not need to be inside a small metal box suspended by cables that could fray and snap at any second... The only elevator she tolerated was the private one to her penthouse in the Marmax building. It was large, well-lit, and stocked with a private telephone and emergency numbers.

"We'll break in a few hours for lunch," Joan stopped and spoke outside the studio door. Carmen was welcome inside, but she would have to stay in the control room with the sound mixer and all the equipment. "I'll introduce you to the guys after that if you want." She held open the door so Carmen could follow after her. She saw her two bandmates and a temporary drummer already in the soundproof, live-room. They weren't jamming, just talking amongst themselves.

Carmen merely nodded, staying in the mixing booth. The sound mixer introduced himself, and she sat next to him. There were worse ways to pass her time than to relax and listen to live music being recorded. Once everyone was settled in, she turned her attention to matters beyond what was going on in the live room.

She pulled out her phone and started doing some research on her newest charge. A quick Google search of the musician's name brought up plenty of results, but her main concern was the images available. She started skimming through the photos of Joan that had been posted online, focusing on candid and paparazzi pictures. She looked for any faces that popped up in more than one picture, since it was a stalker situation on her hands.

Inside the live-room, Joan said hello to the guys and talked with them a bit before they got to work. While she did play guitar, she left it to a team of Russian brothers to cover her acoustic needs most of the time. Rory was an excellent bassist, and Bruce rocked the lead guitar. The percussionist was the only weak link, as he never had an artistic thought to voice. All they had to do was set the music in front of Tony, and the stout man would pull down his prescription sports goggles and play like a machine. Tony would be dependable on stage, but that was it. Joan wasn't expecting any drum solos out of him any time soon. He was – by far – the least passionate drummer she had ever met.

After a small side conversation with Rory away from the microphones, Joan addressed the sound mixer. "Ready for a sound check?" One by one, everyone checked their equipment. Once the sound mixer gave them the okay, the woman informed the group what they were recording first. "Let's do 'Volcano.' I really want to get that done today. Bruce, I want you to come in strong at the second bridge."

The man nodded before he scratched his beard and set his hands in place on his instrument. Joan glanced around to make sure everyone was getting ready. Normally, the only other person in the sound room was Jerry, but he wouldn't come down to check on progress until after lunch. This was Joan's show, and he tried to give her the reins as much as possible.

Joan wasn't nervous about the other presence in the sound booth. Carmen didn't really seem like the fan-girl type. She must have been around enough celebrities to know they were just normal people, mostly. Normal people with money to burn and better access to services and restaurants, but... still people. Besides, Joan was a performer and the recording studio was just a smaller stage.

After counting out the tempo, Joan stared off

into the distance as Rory began the song with a steady, quiet strum of his guitar. Her strong, honeyed voice had won over a great producer, and she put everything she had into it – every time.

> *"Molten rage moves up slowly.*
> *Still don't know what sets you off."*

Right on time, the rest of the band kicked in. They built up to the first verse, and Joan took a breath to expel the confessional lyrics she wrote herself. She was open to suggestions, but she didn't want to rely on some lyricist to write her music for her. They didn't have the same experiences she did, and the kind of artistry she wanted to attain couldn't come from others.

> *"I just taste fire, I feel the flame.*
> *You could try to hurt me but I feel no pain!*
> *I can hear you coming, I watch you blow.*
> *Won't see me running, won't scream no!*
> *You can't tell me I won't do it.*
> *I'll light you up and push through it."*

Singing was a great release for her, and the alternative rock mixed with some new age electronics was a mirror pointed at all the thoughts she had about herself and the world.

> *"I hear you coming, I watch you blow.*
> *Won't see me running, won't scream no!*
> *Don't fucking tell me you're not a volcano!"*

The rest of the song played out with another verse and a repeat of the chorus before dwindling into silence. Rory and Bruce looked proud of themselves, and Joan was bordering on just as happy as the brothers. She still had goosebumps from when Rory had hit those high notes; it happened every time. The song sounded okay, but 'okay' didn't turn records into platinum overnight. As always, she had suggestions.

"Not bad, guys. Not bad. Let's try the bridge in a higher key, all right? One... two... three... four."

14

CHAPTER THREE

From time to time, Carmen glanced up from her phone to make sure the world wasn't ending around them. She could hear the music just fine, but she mostly tuned it out. She'd been inside a studio before, having done some work for other musicians. She was used to hearing pop top 40 songs while inside the booth, so this was definitely different. Not the bad kind of different, though. This was more like what she would listen to.

When lunch rolled around, Joan was ready for a break. Her vocal chords could only take so much, and she had reached her limit for the day. Singing the same power ballad over and over had a tendency to do that. She told the boys that they could stay and work on their own parts if they wanted, but she was done. Joan wasn't going to risk her voice for anything short of a sold-out concert in Times Square.

Joan filed out with the guys. As they left, she introduced each of them to Carmen. No one was shocked that Joan had gotten herself a personal bodyguard, but they were astounded to find out she was a woman. They didn't say anything about it; they just had that flabbergasted look on their faces.

Carmen greeted them in turn, not put off by the surprise on their ugly mugs. She got that reaction more often than she would have liked. She had the experience to back herself up. When push came to shove, that was what mattered.

"I hope you don't have too much of an attachment to cabs," she told Joan as they headed out of the building. "Because I don't like the people I'm working with to take them."

"Then are you going to drive me?" Joan asked. She didn't pose the question in a disrespectful manner like she could have done; she was honestly curious. Celebrities usually didn't drive themselves anywhere because it was dangerous with paparazzi hounds. If photographers found a famous person behind the wheel, they pursued by almost any means. Their recklessness had caused accidents in the past, so at the advice of her manager, Joan stuck to cabs or the professional driving company he recommended.

"Yes," Carmen answered quick and to the point. She had a large vehicle with a high-powered engine and low center of gravity for and good reason: getting her charges out of cabs and in a vehicle that was safer, one that she had control of. After climbing the stairs and heading out the doors of the building, she walked alongside Joan to the parking garage. "Where do you want to go for lunch?" she questioned.

Joan was already craving Thai again, but she vowed to stay away from The Orchid since Stan had shown up there last night. "Um..." Joan scratched the side of her head. She had taken a lot of places off her list of hangouts lately; there wasn't much left. "Your choice, but we don't have to go out. I've got plenty of food in my apartment, if you'd rather."

Carmen pursed her lips, detecting the hesitation in the musician's answer. "You know, you don't have to be afraid of going places," she assured Joan. "I'm good at what I do – nothing will happen." She stepped forward toward her vehicle's passenger side, opening the door for Joan.

Joan eyed Carmen before she got into the vehicle. Aside from some muscle and a 'go-get-em' attitude, she didn't see what made Carmen qualified for the job. But Jerry hired the guard, so that had to mean something.

"I'm not... afraid," she boasted, pulling on her seatbelt. "I'm cautious."

Carmen shut the door and walked around to the driver's side, getting behind the wheel. "You're a shit liar," she stated point blank. "But, I'll be cautious for you – that's my job. I'm just here to provide security so you can get back to your normal routine." She started the vehicle and backed out of the parking place, taking them away from the recording studio.

Joan raised an eyebrow at the blatant statement but she didn't look the other woman in the eye; she couldn't. "So, uh, how does this work? Do I just call you when I need you?" She understood the concept, but who was to say when her body needed guarding? Obviously, Carmen would be around whenever Joan was out publicly, but aside from that...

"Typically, yes, but every situation is different. It really depends on the circumstances," Carmen explained. "Since you're afraid to go out anywhere, the situation has deteriorated *a lot*, and you're going to need me around more than just when you play a gig or go to some event."

Carmen decided to take them out for lunch and see just how uneasy Joan had become about being in public. Since Joan wouldn't talk to her willingly about what was going on, she needed to see it for herself. Carmen continued to speak as she drove, sure of herself in her multitasking.

"Jerry told me where you live, and I know there's security in your building, so you'll be all right when you're at home. Of course, if something comes up and you feel unsafe, you're free to call me. I'll pick you up each morning, take you wherever you need to go, and drop you off at home in the evening."

All in all, that actually didn't sound too bad to Joan. Since she couldn't argue with Carmen's reasoning, she decided to try and get to know the other woman a little better.

"Do you do this a lot? The bodyguard thing?"

Carmen nodded, fishing sunglasses out of the center console. "I got my private officer's license eight months ago, and I've had steady work ever since. I've worked with quite a few celebrities and other big shots since then."

"Oh." Joan had more questions, mostly about who Carmen had worked for in the past, but out of respect she didn't want to pry into the life of other celebrities. After a sudden thought, Joan pulled out her phone. She brought up her list of contacts and began to scroll down. "I don't think I have your number."

Joan had no other Carmens in her contact list, so seeing one already there was a surprise. Jerry must have done it sometime when the singer was busy recording. There were no cell phones allowed in live room; they were all left in the sound mixing booth.

"Never mind." Joan put the device away and watched unfamiliar billboards go by. They weren't going back to her building, that much was clear.

After a few more minutes of driving, they came to a stop outside a row of restaurants and boutiques. Carmen turned off the car and opened up her door as she said, "Wait until I come around and let you out." She slid on a pair of sunglasses while she walked around the vehicle. Honestly, she didn't know how well Joan would take to her methods and the little nuances like waiting for her to put a barrier between the musician and the public. Joan would just have to get used to it.

By not being allowed to open her own door, Joan felt like a child. She would have said something about it, but she reminded herself that Carmen would walk away if any attitude came to the surface again. She had yet to see Stan at the studio, so the chances he had followed her here were pretty slim. Or maybe they were big; maybe she hadn't seen her stalker because he didn't want her to, yet. Joan stepped out of the SUV when the world opened up to her and waited for Carmen to lead the way.

Scanning the area behind dark shades, Carmen's glare came through in the way she held herself as a muscle in her jaw twitched. She turned to lead the way into the stucco-covered restaurant and held the door for Joan. The place was a nice Mexican restaurant, full of handmade furnishings and accentuated with thematic music. She came inside right behind Joan to guide her over to a table so they could sit.

Joan tried to be polite company. Of the three P's, this was where her public mannerisms needed to come to the forefront. She took her spot at a booth along the back wall and quietly waited for Carmen to strike up conversation or for one of the staff to come by. She could tell that a couple of people at the table across from them recognized her, but they held off on approaching her and went about their meals. Joan didn't mind it; the autographs, pictures, and attention. Most people were respectful and said their 'please' and 'thank you's.

Carmen slid her sunglasses off, hooking them on the front of her black tank top. A waiter came through and took their drink orders, gawking a little over the singer he got to wait on, before heading off again. He mentioned something about playing celebrity bingo with the rest of staff and how he got to put a chip over Celebrity Musician with Original Band Members. Joan held her tongue about replacing Tony and the fact that she wasn't part of a band. She was *Joan Devintia*.

"So, are you going to tell me about what's

going on, or am I going to have to guess everything?" Carmen questioned over her menu.

Joan sighed, distractedly looking at the porcelain figurine salt and pepper shakers between them. She really didn't want to talk about it here and with someone who was still a stranger to her. How could she be sure Carmen wouldn't just sell the information or something? Jerry had hired Carmen, she reminded herself, and that was pretty much a gold stamp of approval.

"It started over a month ago. This guy kept... showing up at places. Which, you know," Joan fussed with her hair, sweeping away a lock that had fallen across her undercut, "isn't that crazy. While I was on tour with Despite Darkness, people followed the band across the country. The roadies came to every show and got backstage when they could. But this guy isn't like them. He's never approached for an autograph or just to say hi-" Joan had to stop talking. Paranoia was playing tricks on her, making her feel the ghostly sensation of her stalker's presence when he wasn't around. That was why she didn't like to talk about this; why she tried not to even think of it.

Carmen wasn't the best with bedside manners – the military had that effect on some. But, she could understand Joan's discomfort. Obviously, this whole ordeal was quite hard on her, and it was her job to let the singer know that everything would be all right.

"Hey, it's okay," she said while pushing the salt shaker on the other side of the pepper where she felt like it belonged. "While I'm around, you don't have to worry about him. But these are the things I need to know, so I can do my job better. A lot of the people in this field are reactive – they wait for shit to happen. I'd rather be pro-active and stop anything from ever happening."

She doubted her words would be very comforting, considering Joan knew so little about her and her work thus far. "You know, the big celebs have their bodyguards that have been with them for years – hulking dudes that look like they could pull a semi with their teeth. But sometimes, they still need a little extra help to keep things from getting blown out of proportion, or they need some extra security for an event. You didn't hear about Tina Wilson's stalker last month, did you? Nobody has, because I got in, took care of him, and got back out under the radar. Priya Dhar was one of my first jobs, she was going to Tokyo and some of the people were rabid over there. Nobody got within ten feet of her if she didn't want them to. Just last week, I was with Megan Wolfe at a premiere in L.A."

Hearing such big names was a comfort to Joan. The waiter came by before she could say anything else. As he passed out drinks, Joan began to lose her nerve. She was beginning to doubt her own story and her own uneasy feelings. She couldn't be popular enough to warrant the same bodyguard that worked with A-listers.

"I don't want to come off as some unapproachable bitch to my fans. Maybe he's just shy, and I'm overreacting."

"Trust me, if your gut is telling you something is wrong... then something is wrong," Carmen replied. This was the first time she had worked with someone who was just breaking out into stardom. The others she had worked with were used to the attention – the good and the bad, and just wanted it dealt with. "I can't tell you how many times gut instinct saved my life and the lives of the people around me. I don't doubt that this guy is following you. It's pretty obvious if you can't even talk about it or go places that you normally go." Carmen set her menu aside, ready to order when their waiter came back for them. She wasn't sure why she had pretended to read from it; she always ordered the same food.

Joan pursed her lips, her situation so blatantly set out before her. To hear that Carmen had been in many life and death situations seemed like an interesting change of topic.

"What did you do that was so dangerous before this?" Joan placed her menu on the end of the table. "If I can ask that is," she added quickly.

Carmen reached up and tugged the chain around her neck, pulling her dog tags out from where they'd been resting under her tank top. They were missing the silencers – the rubber cases that kept them from making noise. She didn't like the feel of them against her skin.

"I'm a Marine. I'm in my last year and a half of inactive duty."

"Oh." Joan glanced at the metal jewelry before looking back into Carmen's dark eyes. "You're going back then?" If Carmen was in the Marines, she was probably a war veteran as well, what with the country constantly at war. Joan couldn't imagine being a part of the military, though she would gladly entertain the troops if such an opportunity to presented itself.

"Only if they need me to," Carmen answered dryly.

The waiter came and took their food orders, picking up the menus before disappearing once more. Joan requested something simple, not wanting to tax her diet too badly. Out of respect for the soldier, she let the topic slip away.

"So, what did you think of my music?" she teasingly asked. Joan really didn't know what else to talk about and while she wasn't usually narcissistic, it was fun to play the part sometimes.

"You've got a good voice," Carmen answered, circumventing the actual question.

Joan raised her eyebrows, noticing what Carmen did and didn't say about her music. "Let me guess... you're more of a country fan?" she joked, knowing well enough that was something Carmen was *not*. The station playing in the SUV was 96.6, MuseX, which usually played rap and other urban contemporary music.

"Ah, you caught me," Carmen played along with a smile before shaking her head. At home, she tended to listen to more rap, but on deployment it was heavy metal that got her blood pumping. "So, were you one of those kids that had a microphone in their hand when they were two?"

Joan grinned back at Carmen. "No. I went to Hollywood to live the cliché dream of becoming of an actress, but as it turned out – I can't act to save my life. I can sing though. I started getting small gigs in bars, doing all sorts of covers. You name the song, I probably know it."

Their food arrived on steaming hot plates, which the server warned them about before he left again. Joan picked up a fork and took a bite. She was much more relaxed than she had been before, and it didn't take an under-the-table prescription to do it.

"I figured that if I was going to make singing into a career, then I better start writing my own music. I've been in love with it ever since."

Carmen nodded as she listened to Joan's story and started eating. She'd gotten a platter of authentic tacos – not like the ones purchased for a dollar at some shitty national chain Tex-Mex restaurant.

"You're set to release a full CD soon, aren't you?" she questioned.

"Yeah," Joan answered between bites. "We're gonna finish recording this week, do a music video after that. Then the CDs will be manufactured and out the door. It usually takes months to do all that, but Jerry is one of the best producers in the business. I'm not only one he manages, either."

"He's called me before. He takes good care of his people." Granted, this was the first time he'd called Carmen in the middle of the damn night, but that just went to show how far he would go for his talent. Most agents did the bare minimum to get the most money possible. Jerry actually took an interest in his clients.

Joan smiled at the memory of their morning when Jerry reprimanded her for being late and then rude on top of that. He was a good guy, if not a little tough with his talent. The two women went through the rest of the meal with similar small talk. Joan tried to keep her blue eyes to herself, but she did find herself looking for Stan once or twice between trying wrestle a sudden infatuation with Carmen's eyebrows.

Joan offered to pay. She told Carmen it was to make amends for her attitude that morning. On their way out, it looked like someone had finally gotten the courage to approach the singer before she disappeared forever. A couple of teenagers who could have passed for Abercrombie and Fitch models got up from their table and called out to her.

"Joan? I'm sorry to bother you-"

She turned around and tried to smile. They weren't disturbing her at all; she was just weary of people approaching her from behind.

Carmen stepped closer to the singer, moving slightly in front of the other woman. She crossed her arms over her chest as she looked the pair over.

"Make it quick," she told them shortly. "She's on a schedule." Even if Joan wanted to be nice to her fans, it was a bodyguard's duty to be the one to keep them from taking up too much time.

24

Joan glanced at Carmen before looking back to her fans. She didn't want to undermine her new bodyguard in front of the public, but she didn't like lying when it wasn't necessary. The couple probably just wanted an autograph or something.

The young woman nodded and spoke quickly, whether that was out of nerves or respect of what Carmen said was up for debate. "I'm Marissa," she introduced herself, "and this is Tom. I just wanted to say that I love, love, love Frostbite. I saw you in Phoenix when you opened for Despite Darkness, and I'd never heard you before. You were just amazing."

Joan smiled at the pair, white teeth shining through at the praise. "Goodness. Thank you. I appreciate hearing that so much," she honestly told the fan.

"Do you think I could get a picture with you?"

"Absolutely," Joan answered without hesitation.

The teenager buzzed with anticipation and sported a goofy smile. She fished out her phone and handed it to the young man nearby. He was already pointing it at the celebrity and her company by the time Joan got close to the fan. She wrapped a hand around the woman, politely keeping it on the fan's shoulder as she smiled toward the phone. The picture was over and done with in a literal flash. Technology made it so easy these days for everyone to be a photographer. It certainly made the fans happier when they met someone.

"Thank you! Oh my god, this is so awesome. It's going straight to my Twitter," the teen told the star.

Joan's smile faltered a bit, but she kept her mind in the present. "I have to get going, but it was great to meet you, Marissa and Tom."

25

Carmen kept a close eye on the two fans, but they were harmless. She'd seen the glance she got from Joan at the start of impromptu meeting, but she was doing her job. The singer was going to have to get used to that. Once the stalker was dealt with, she'd ease up on the people who approached her charge, but until that point they were going by her rules.

CHAPTER FOUR

When the photo op was done, Carmen turned and ushered the singer out of the restaurant. Autographs and quick pictures she would allow, but they weren't going to stand around and talk forever. She led Joan back over to the SUV, opening the passenger door for her.

Joan got into the black vehicle and withdrew her cell phone. She had no missed calls or texts. With a few motions on the screen, she opened the Twitter app and saw several notifications. At first, checking social websites was just fuel for her ego. Most of the "fuck me!!!1!" comments were flattering, especially when they were from women, but there were plenty of ridiculous users in her feed that put her off being married to social media. Chewing on her bottom lip, she saw the post Marissa had talked about making.

> *just met @joandcvintia totes fangirling rn instagram.com/p/BEbnhtVnAOL/ #amazing #bae*

Joan also saw that someone had favorited it already. The singer couldn't be sure that Stan had a Twitter profile, but if he did, the Twitter handle @joaneternal was hard to misinterpret. The only reason she visited sites like Twitter and Facebook anymore was to watch and monitor her pages for this kind of activity. For his activity. The mysterious user never tweeted anything; he never posted on her wall. He liked and favorited within minutes of postings, and it was entirely creepy. The singer was more than ready to go back to her apartment now.

Carmen went to the driver's side of the vehicle and got in. When they were back on the road, Carmen glanced over at the singer and noticed that something seemed off. Joan looked uneasy and uncomfortable in her own skin.

"Everything okay?" she asked, turning her attention back to the street.

Nixing the app, Joan placed her iPhone back in her purse. "I'm ready to go home," she answered, squeezing the bridge of her nose to fight off a pestering bout of nausea. "It's been a long week," she excused herself. Even though it was only Thursday and she took Monday off, she had accomplished a lot.

"You know... if you're not honest with me, and don't tell me what's going on, it hinders what I'm able to do for you." Carmen was already heading in the direction of Joan's building, so she didn't have to change their course.

Joan set her jaw as she stared out the passenger window. After a few moments of counting lampposts, she loosened her tongue with a little fire. The singer wasn't about to send her bodyguard after some random internet user on a hunch.

"When I see him again, you'll be the first to know." Joan mentally got on herself for saying 'when' not 'if.' She couldn't be thinking like this, like she was some prize at the end of the map that – sooner or later – was going to be dug up and plundered.

Carmen didn't offer the singer a response. If Joan was going to be uncooperative, that was her prerogative. It turned her into a player on the sideline, and while Carmen would do her job as effectively as she could, it would be harder. She drove in silence, and they made it to the building without incident. Newly parked, she got out of the SUV and walked around to let Joan out of the vehicle.

Joan had placed her hand on the handle of the car door before she remembered that she was to be let out, like some kind of fugitive. Celebrities were prisoners in a way, trapped between two very public eyes most of the time. She knew she had to watch everything she did so she didn't offend or alienate anyone, and that included the hired help. If she pissed off Carmen too badly, the Marine might do more than just walk away.

Joan led the way toward her building. Turning to Carmen inside the lobby, she asked, "Do you want to come up?"

Carmen nodded. "If that's all right with you. I'd like to make sure everything checks out." She did that with everyone who was dealing with a stalker situation. Stalkers weren't to be taken lightly – some could be fairly harmless, but others had mental shortfalls that could make them dangerous. If this creep had been following her for a month, he was likely the latter.

"It doesn't bother me," Joan reassured Carmen. This was one of the reasons she had requested a female bodyguard. She wanted someone she could welcome into the intimacies of her life if she had to, someone who would understand which bad days were because of PMS – someone who wasn't a dick because they had one.

Joan swiped her card at a private elevator and walked in first. It was Jerry who actually owned the penthouse part of the building, thanks to an old deal amongst friends. The manager left it open for his talent when they needed a new place, and right now – it was Joan's.

She took her usual place against one of the sidewalls and waited until Carmen joined her before pressing the button to ascend. The elevator didn't lead right into the penthouse, but let out at a short hallway where the stairs also connected. With the swift turn of a key, Joan was inside one of the only places she truly felt safe anymore. For the past couple of weeks, she had been locking the door again after she entered. She forfeited the compulsion this time. Carmen didn't need any more evidence of the singer's paranoia.

The apartment was large and well-furnished. Everything was some varied dark shade – between deep blues, wine-like reds, and straight up black. Some of the furniture and amenities belonged to the hotel, but Joan tried to make it look like a rocker lived here. She had a pool table; her collection of albums; and classy, framed pictures of guitars. Her own white Les Paul was resting against the wall in the living room where she left it last night. She went to grab it up and place it somewhere safer, handling it with care. She might fiddle with some notes later, but she didn't feel like playing much right now. Instead, she put it in a closet next to her saltwater aquarium.

Joan took good care of her spotted seahorses and only purchased the best she could afford for them. Her favorite was the buttermilk female, Sunshine, who liked to hitch herself to the red sea grass toward the front of the tank. Joan didn't really have enough time or energy for a commitment bigger than her hundred-gallon tank.

Carmen stepped into the space behind Joan and took everything in. At first glance, everything looked to be copacetic – except for the fact that the DVD's in Joan's media center weren't organized alphabetically and there were about a hundred picks lying around in various places. A first look was never good enough, though. Fine details were found in a more scrutinizing inspection. Carmen looked at all the doors and windows she could find without intruding beyond the living room she had been welcomed into. Joan's movies definitely weren't sorted at all.

"Do you mind if I take a walk around?" she questioned after a moment. Of course, if Joan didn't want her to, she would stay in place. Familiarizing herself with the penthouse and finding any vulnerabilities would certainly be beneficial.

"Go on ahead," Joan said as she checked on her aquatic friends.

Aside from the living room, there were two bedrooms, two bathrooms, a full kitchen, plenty of closet space, and one hell of a balcony. Joan spent a lot of her time out there in the evenings, staring at the black ocean and thinking about life. There wasn't a lot for her to do while she had company around, so she poured herself a drink of flavored, German liquor after she determined that her seahorses were fine. She doubted Carmen would want a drink while she was 'on the job,' but she still planned to offer.

Carmen walked through the penthouse which was about a hundred times nicer than her own apartment. She checked windows and scouted for anything that could present itself as a vulnerability. She highly doubted the stalker would have access to C-4 to put a charge on the other side of an inner wall, so that wouldn't be a concern. That meant the only places she had to worry about were the windows and the balcony.

Bottle and clean glass in hand, Joan found Carmen. "Peppermint schnapps?"

When Joan spoke behind her, Carmen turned to face the singer. "No, thanks," she answered. She wasn't much for liquor unless it was straight whiskey or tequila, or beer.

Joan helped herself to the bottle and glass, pouring out another serving before drinking it down. She was in no way, shape, or form about to get drunk before five o'clock, but she didn't mind taking the edge off. The alcohol burned her throat but the peppermint flavoring soothed it as the sting wore away.

She didn't know exactly what Carmen was looking for, but she was getting fearful that the woman might find something. Joan would lose her shit if Carmen found a hidden camera or something else to that effect.

Carmen continued her meticulous search until she'd gotten all the way through the apartment. Nothing seemed out of the ordinary, and there was no outer fire escape for someone to climb. At least up to this point, no one unwanted had gotten into the penthouse.

"Looks good," she announced. "Just to be on the safe side, I want you to keep your door locked, okay? I'm sure you know this already, but don't open it for anyone you don't know. I live about ten minutes away, so I can get here fast if I need to – traffic gods willing."

Relief flooded Joan as the bodyguard gave the all clear. She set the bottle of schnapps down on a nearby counter and tried to breathe a little easier. It dawned on her that she hadn't really thanked Carmen for what she was doing. Sure, she was paying the bodyguard, or Jerry was, but the monetary compensation didn't satisfy Joan's need to show her appreciation. Carmen was giving her the one thing she couldn't get for herself: peace of mind.

"Thank you. Thanks for doing this," she spoke as rapidly as her fan had done earlier.

Carmen smiled as she looked over at the obviously reassured singer. "You don't have to thank me," she said. "This is all a part of the job. I'll be on call all day, every day. So if you need anything, you have my number – even if it's the middle of the night and you heard a strange noise." The only thing that she wouldn't do was act like an assistant. She was here for security, not Starbucks.

Joan's heart swelled at thought of having someone to call in the middle of night for no other reason than to investigate the strange noises of imaginary ghosts. She should have listened to Jerry sooner; she should have known Carmen sooner. Maybe she wouldn't be in the position she was now if she had.

"All right," Joan confirmed that she'd heard and understood. "I'm not going anywhere else tonight, so if you want to head home – you can."

"I don't want you going anywhere without me knowing. As of this morning, I'm your personal security, chauffeur, and your shadow. If you need to go somewhere, call me first," Carmen ordered. She figured giving up so much privacy would be an adjustment for Joan, but it was necessary in order to keep her safe. "If you're sure you'll be okay for the night, I'll head out."

"Oh, wait." Joan left swiftly and returned almost as quickly with an extra card and key for the penthouse. Before she handed them over, she met Carmen's serious gaze.

"This is my spare set; the only spare set," she clarified. "Please don't lose them." There was a lot of blind trust in the act. Joan hoped that Carmen appreciated that. The owner of the building was the only other person who could access the penthouse, and he was under strict legal guidance to enter without permission only under extreme circumstances.

"Don't worry. I wouldn't be very good security if I lost people's keys." Carmen took the offered key and card. "I'm here to watch your back, not give someone else access to it." She slid the items into the safety of one of her pockets, then felt to make sure they were secure there. She was always careful when given the keys to someone else's apartment – or mansion, in some cases.

Joan walked Carmen to the door and bid the other woman a good night. Maybe she was feeling the booze – or maybe she'd been alone for a little too long – but at the entryway, Joan's eyes lingered on Carmen's figure while Carmen wasn't looking. It would get her a certain kind of press if she was ever seen dating another woman, but Joan didn't give a fuck. She was absolutely the type to pursue who she wanted despite their gender. Being wrote off as a dyke might hurt the career of an actress, but as a rocker – it was kind of expected of her to err on the wrong side of society's norms. Besides, her bisexual label wasn't as important as her record label.

Joan averted her gaze out of respect and uncertainty that she should be ogling the woman, after an infatuation with Carmen's biceps was added to her attraction to Carmen's sharp eyebrows. They had a working relationship now; anything else would be unprofessional and not to mention cliché. She just liked that Carmen made her feel safe; that was all.

Thankfully, Carmen didn't notice that the singer's gaze lingered. She was too distracted by her job to think about anything else. No one had ever accused her of not being dedicated – whether it was the military or the private sector now.

"Good night," she replied. "I'll see you in the morning." After that, she left it to Joan to lock the door behind her.

On her way out of the Marmax building, Carmen stopped by the security desk to see if they'd had any problems lately. They chatted a bit, and she learned nothing suspicious had been going on, and no one who shouldn't have been there had turned up. That was a good sign. Either the guy didn't know where Joan lived, or he didn't have the balls to show up yet.

With that taken care of, Carmen went home. Her single bedroom, barely 500 square foot apartment was much like a broom closet compared to the singer's penthouse. But Carmen wasn't one for living outside of her means. The apartment she had now felt like a mansion after living in barracks on a single wide bed for four years. And after living on MREs, keeping a stash of unused mini-bottles of Tabasco sauce, and hoarding packets of sugar – real food was a blessing not to be squandered.

Inside her apartment, the first thing she did was flip over the brass deadbolt. She went into the kitchen, which was only separated from the living room by a half wall on one side, and started emptying her pockets. Each movement was methodical – first the handgun from the holster at her back, then the holster, followed by her wallet, keys, and finally the card and key for Joan's penthouse. She laid down each item carefully, making sure it lined up perfectly where she wanted it. Though she tried not to show it outside the confines of her home, Carmen dealt with mild to sometimes moderate OCD.

Everything in the apartment was in its right place, and not a centimeter off of where it should have been. It gave Carmen a sense of order and control, where she hadn't been afforded that during the time of her deployments.

With nothing more to do for the evening, she went to the fridge and grabbed herself a beer, popping the top off and flicking it in the trash. She went into the living room and sat down, pulling out her laptop to do a bit more research since her phone could only do so much.

Carmen turned in rather late, having spent much of the night looking up her newest client online. She went through dozens of articles and looked through more pictures. She even filtered through Joan's Twitter account, looking for anything that was a telltale sign. Her fans' online presence was vast and quite active, so it was hard to see if there was anything out of the ordinary.

When she finally did go to bed, everything in the apartment was turned off and she grabbed her handgun to take with her into the bedroom. She placed it in the drawer of the bedside table, then went to the bathroom to brush her teeth, before dressing down to a tank and pair of boxers. The full size bed offered more than enough room for her and, even though it wasn't technically a luxury, it was one of the few she allowed herself.

Across the city, Joan had spent a good hour on her balcony watching the sun melt into calm waters. There were perks to her perks, and this incredible view was one of them. Up there, Joan felt like she could see the world and it couldn't see her. Even the planes overhead were too high to make out the lone woman lounging on a rooftop.

When the singer turned in, she set her television to one of the entertainment channels and watched late night reruns. Between tattoo shows, she fell asleep on the couch – too tired to get to bed. Lately, she needed the noise and company the TV offered, fake as it was. If she could hear people arguing on-screen about tattoo placement, then she couldn't hear footsteps off-screen.

As usual, Joan woke around five in the morning and wandered to her mattress. She barely had the energy to kick off her pants as she lay in bed. The noise of paid programming could still be heard as Joan drifted off again. Her phone alarm would go off at eight AM. When it did, she would rise, shower, and worry about the new dangers of the day.

CHAPTER FIVE

Deeply embedded into routine, Carmen woke up a minute before her alarm went off and got up. Her day started the same way as every other – after getting dressed, she went to the gym for an hour. The weight-heavy workout was followed by a protein-packed breakfast while she caught up on the day's early news. Jerry had e-mailed her a rough, typical schedule of Joan's day, so she would have an idea of what to expect.

By 8:30 AM, she was heading out the door to go pick up the singer. She sent Joan a text message, letting the musician know that she was on her way.

At the threshold of the penthouse suite, Joan had to do a double-take when her phone chirped at her. No one but Jerry texted her this early, but that wasn't the name on her phone. It was Carmen; Joan had almost forgotten. She was two seconds away from walking out the door and hailing herself a cab. It was a good thing she hadn't gotten that far. Carmen probably would have had some strong words about that.

Instead of leaving, Joan turned back around and watched her seahorses swim in their sloppy, feeble way until Carmen arrived. Today was just another day in the studio, but the night... Friday nights were usually spent partying. She had several friends downtown and the Russian duo, Rory and Bruce, were always up for a kegger or more.

Carmen picked up Joan about fifteen minutes after having sent the text to the singer. Maybe it wasn't totally necessary to lock Joan down so thoroughly, since the stalker hadn't showed up at her home yet. Still, it was always better to be safe than sorry.

Joan stopped by Jerry's office to say hello and discuss a little business. Since she was on time today, she'd be waiting on the rest of the band to arrive. Jerry was pleased to talk shop with his newest star, but before it was over, he grabbed a stack of sealed envelopes held together with a rubber band.

"Your fanmail this week, Ms. Devintia."

"Sweet." Joan took the bundle and placed it in her purse. "Thanks, Jerry." Handwritten letters were about the only interaction with her fans she fully engaged in anymore. Tweets and Facebook posts were all well and good, but that people would take the time to write these heartfelt pieces was like a glance at the past. Jerry told her that back in the day his clients would get a hundred letters a day, sometimes more. Now, all of that attention was deflected to impersonal pixels on a screen. It was a blessing of sorts. The letters gave Joan real insight into how the public felt about her, and she could avoid all the trolls and pervs who ruined it for the real fans online.

Joan excused herself, expecting security to follow her out. Carmen had been standing idly by, looking out the window of Jerry's office while the singer and her manager talked about the trade. When Joan was ready to leave, she turned to go with her. As Joan hit the door, Jerry called out to Carmen.

"Ms. Savedra, will you hang back for a moment, please? There's something I would like to discuss with you."

"Go ahead," Carmen told Joan. "I'll be down in ten minutes, tops." After the singer left, Carmen approached Jerry's desk. "What's up?"

Jerry didn't answer until Joan was gone and the heavy door was shut behind her. The manager took a deep breath before giving his full attention to the bodyguard.

"I hope Joan has stopped being difficult, and since you're still here, I'll assume she has. But-" The aged man pulled out another, thinner stack of envelopes and papers from under his desk. This time the envelopes were cut open with a sharp edge, but their matching notes and papers were still tucked inside.

"The situation is probably more extreme than she's told you." The manager set the inch-high stack on his desk before and pushed them toward Carmen. "I've been keeping these from Joan for the past two months. They're from her stalker, whoever it is." At first, Jerry let the envelopes without return addresses slip by him, and he gave them to the singer. But when Joan started to get a few of them a week, Jerry took notice. With the first letter he opened, he knew this unknown sender had the potential to turn into what he had become. The manager had seen it all before.

"I've already pulled my strings to get Forensics to look at them, but they didn't find any fingerprints. She gets two or three of them a week, but the contents of the letters are... sporadic. I'm sure you'll see it for yourself." Jerry was worried for his newest star and it showed. "Whatever you do with these, I'd prefer it if Joan didn't know about them. She's young," he reasoned with the other woman. "She doesn't have the poise and experience to deal with something like this on her own."

Carmen sighed, having hoped it wouldn't have gotten to this point. She cursed internally as she reached out to grab the small stack of letters. She leafed through the stack, but didn't try to read them at the moment. That would wait until later, when she was at home and wouldn't have to worry about Joan walking in and seeing that she had them.

"I'll look into this," she assured the man. "I would recommend not opening any more, just give them straight to me. If you can avoid it, don't touch them with your bare hands. I've got a friend that may be able to help with this. Is there anything else going on that I should know about?"

Jerry could easily accommodate Carmen's wishes, but he didn't know what she could find that he didn't. He tried his best to take care of his clients, he really did. They weren't just access to his paycheck, they were young people living their dreams and he cherished that.

"I'm sorry, Ms. Savedra. If there's more, I don't know it. Joan only told me that someone was following her."

"Okay. Thank you for not waiting to give me these." Carmen slid the letters into one of the deep pockets of her black cargo pants, where they would safely rest and avoid Joan's notice. "If anything else comes up, I'm the first to know, all right?"

"Of course," Jerry nodded. He was ready to let the woman leave, but he gave her some parting words to think about. "Joan has a remarkable voice, but what's happening now will leave a mark on her career. Protect her," he whispered.

"Don't you worry. I'm going to take good care of her, and I'll do it as quietly as possible so the press doesn't start hounding her about it." After the assurances, Carmen turned to walk out of the office – and that was when she nearly collided with tall, tan, and pretentious.

"Oh, excuse me. I didn't know the cleaning crew worked this shift."

Carmen ground her teeth at the young man trying to get past her. His sandy-colored hair and green polo shirt went well with his privilege. Before she could decide what to do with the micro-aggression, Jerry intervened.

"Kevin, Ms. Savedra is Joan's new bodyguard. If you would have been to work on time yesterday, you would have met her then."

The man's jaw dropped as he realized his mistake. "Jesus. Sorry, Ms. Savedra, I had no idea-"

"It's fine," Carmen said, stopping him from completing an apology she'd heard too many times to believe anymore. Nothing about casual racism was fine, but she wasn't about to jeopardize her new job over it.

Jerry shook his head. "Kevin Lewis is my assistant," he informed Carmen.

"Right." Carmen ignored her pride and shook Kevin's hand. The man looked like he would rather be anywhere but here. He made his escape quick enough as soon as Carmen made space for him. As the office door began to close behind him, she heard Kevin plead his case.

"About my tardiness yesterday... I had a late night- "

The door clicked shut. Carmen was getting toward the tail end of the ten-minute deadline, so she headed down to the studio.

It didn't bother Joan that she was without her bodyguard. Inside the studio, she had plenty of people looking out for her, including the Russian duo. Inside the live room, as they set up their instruments, Rory and Bruce made small talk while the microphones were still off.

"Where's your bodyguard?" Bruce asked Joan.

"Talking to Jerry, I think."

"I didn't know women were bodyguards," Rory added as he plugged in his guitar. "That's hot, dude. She could guard my body any day, if you know what I'm saying."

Joan rolled her eyes and popped Rory on the head with a nearby drumstick. "Everyone knows what you're saying, but don't let Carmen hear you say that. She's a Marine, too."

Rory's jaw dropped. "That's even hotter," he whispered in awe.

The singer shook her head as she turned on her mic. "New topic," she told the boys. "Are we going to Jessica's tonight?"

Bruce whined. "Oh, come on. We've gone there the past three Friday's in a row. Her house is great, but I want that club scene. I want bottle service and hot babes on the floor. Let's go to Prestige."

Joan bit her lip as Rory and Tony agreed with the guitarist. "All right, all right," she conceded. Prestige was not a place Joan felt welcome anymore, but maybe things would go differently this time. She had Carmen to watch her back now.

The bodyguard walked down and joined the sound mixer in the booth, taking the seat she'd had the day before. It was a good thing she hadn't heard Rory's comments, otherwise she would have had some stern words for him. Instead, she came in, right on time to hear them chatting about where they wanted to go that night.

The thought of a club was already fraying her thin patience. It was the absolute worst place for her to try and do her job. So many people, so many things that could go wrong. But, as she had said, she wanted to keep Joan's life as normal as possible. The life of a rocker included going to some club, drinking, and dancing.

Today she had nothing to do, but listen to the music that was being recorded. So she settled in to get comfortable while she waited.

Joan was calm in the beginning of the session, but as the minutes ticked by – she grew more nervous. Prestige was one of the first places Joan had actually seen her tie-wearing stalker and knew he wasn't just

42

watching her because she had a pretty face. None of the guys were aware of Joan's problem and she wanted to keep it that way. The fewer people who knew, the better. Not that she didn't trust them; she didn't want Stan to define her like that.

Instead of going out to lunch, the group voted for pizza and Jerry obliged from his office upstairs. Around noon, he brought the food down and told Carmen that she could help herself or she was welcome to take a lunch. Joan wouldn't be going anywhere and she was relatively safe in the studio with everyone around.

It was a late day in the studio, so when seven o'clock rolled around Joan didn't hang around the guys and stuck by Carmen's side. At the SUV, Joan stopped the other woman to talk.

"Is it cool with you if we go out with the boys? They want to go to a club tonight," she informed Carmen, unaware that she already knew. Some part of Joan was secretly hoping that Carmen would shoot her down, but at the same time, she wanted to live a normal life.

"I heard," Carmen told her with a nod. Prestige was nicer than other places, so it weeded out some of the riff raff, but it wouldn't stop a determined individual. Carmen would still have to be on high alert, and not let Joan stray too far from her side. A club was a good place for an obsessed fan to get close to their celebrity infatuation.

"We can go," she informed Joan. "But I don't want you to leave my sight, okay? That's my only rule when it comes to clubbing. Well, that and not leaving with some stranger, but I figure that's usually pretty self-explanatory."

Joan perked a thin eyebrow at Carmen. "What kind of girl do you take me for?" she teased. She wasn't really into going home with strangers or

43

bringing them back to her place. She was out to dance and have fun, not foster a scandalous reputation.

Carmen gave Joan an empty, unfeeling grin. She shook her head as she opened up the passenger door for the singer. Once Joan was settled inside, Carmen shut the door and walked around to get in the driver's seat.

"Do you need to go home and get ready for club?" she questioned as she started the vehicle.

"Yes, please." After recording all day, Joan's hair was a mess from constantly running her fingers through it. Plus, she wanted to change into something that said she was looking to go home with someone that night, even though she wouldn't follow through.

"Um, this isn't the way home," Joan said, eyebrows knit in confusion as the SUV pulled onto a foreign stretch of road.

Carmen raised two fingers in the air and ticked them off. "You remember rule number one: you let me drive," she reminded Joan. "Rule number two: you have to vary your routine. Never do the same thing every day, never take the same route two days in a row."

"Hm, I guess I have a lot to learn."

"Follow my rules, and you'll be fine. I haven't lost a client. Yet."

At her penthouse, Joan told Carmen to make herself at home wherever she pleased. She was welcome to turn on the TV or go out to the balcony, because it would probably take Joan a good hour to get ready. At least. Joan's black nail polish needed to be redone and there was other grooming to attend to.

Carmen nodded and settled herself on the couch, turning the TV on for some background noise – and cover. After Joan left the room, she reached down into her pocket and pulled the letters out. She had planned on waiting to read them until she was in

44

the seclusion of her own apartment, but since the singer was going out somewhere that they could encounter this guy, Carmen needed an idea of what the stalker was like. She had read some twisted fan mail before, and assumed it would be of a similar type.

Oh, how she was wrong.

Ms. Devintia,

I saw you open for Despite Darkness tonight again. You were like a dream. I wish you would have been on stage longer. I tried to get backstage to meet you, but the goons working security wouldn't let me. I simply wanted to tell you that you're an angel — my angel.
I can't wait to see you again.

Ms. Devintia,

I saw you in concert again tonight. You are truly amazing.

You looked at me during the show, right at the eclipse of Volcano. It was beautiful, magnetic, like Fate put the spotlights on you and me, and there wasn't a single other worthy soul in that entire auditorium. Did you feel our connection?

I did. I will see you in Salt Lake City in a few days. Will you see me?

Joan,

     We match now. I walked into a tattoo shop, out of the blue, and I was compelled to mark myself in way you would appreciate. My bicep now says F☺CK, just like yours. Do you know what I think it means? I think it means the world can go fuck itself, and it can do it with a smile! That's what I'm going to do. I'm going to tell the world to go fuck itself with a shit-eating grin.

Joan,

     Your fire is burning me alive and I want to know where it comes from. I want to know why you take away the pain.
     Will you tell me?

Joan,

> *You sound and look so lonely while you perform. Don't worry, my angel, you won't be lonely much longer.*
> *I quit my job so there's nothing keeping me away anymore. Can you believe it? Those fuckers looked so relieved. I said I'm leaving, and they held open the door.*
> *I feel so free. Free to love you like no one has ever loved you, and you'll never feel alone again.*

Dear Joan,

Your voice is so sweet. If I could just hear you say my name once, I could die happy.

Joan, my love,

I saw you at The Orchid tonight. You looked so beautiful. I wish you noticed me.

Joan,

You're so beautiful. Not the kind of beautiful that other plastic, so-called celebrities claim to be.
Your voice, the words that come straight from your soul... I can feel you speaking to me. It inspires me.

God damn woman. You fucking bitch.
I'm going to enjoy it when I get my hands on you and
watch the life drain from your face.

Joan,

> *My sweet, I'm so sorry for my last letter. Please forgive me. I don't know what got into me. I promise it won't happen again.*
> *I love you.*

Joan,

     You should stop taking pictures with people. I see them posted all over the internet.
     It's disgusting. You're disgusting, you attention whore. Don't you know how much that hurts me?
     Oh, but I can't stay angry with you, my angel.

It feels like… It feels like there are these worms squirming in my head. Crawling. Digging.

Do your fans feel like worms, Joan? Do they press in around you with their slimy bodies, trying to bury themselves in you? Do they want to feel your insides?

I know what those worms feel like. I can take care of them for you. I'll drown them. Yes, drown them and wait until their bodies wash up, then crush them like the little worms they are. There will be nothing left but blood and guts, and I'll make a cake out of them for you.

My Angel,

I bought something for you today, I'm so excited.
You'll love it. The blade is already polished and ready for you.
Oh, my dear, how exquisite it will look against your throat.

Do angels bleed?
I hope so.

Joan,

My sweet. My love. My angel.
I haven't seen you out much lately. It's because you don't want anyone knowing about us, isn't it? You want to keep our love a secret.
I understand. Truly, I do.
Don't worry, I'll take care of anyone who tries to get in our way.
Nothing can keep me from you.

After that last note, Carmen set them down in her lap and reached up to rub the bridge of her nose. Aside from the demented, tormented spiral of mental spew – the fact that half of the 'letters' were written on recipe cards was incredibly off-putting. There was nothing quite like reading about crushing worms next to the baking instructions for caramel-apple cheesecake.

"Creepy ass, motherfucker," she said quietly to herself.

This had progressed quickly and was far worse than she had imagined. This stalker was bi-polar at best, and schizophrenic, completely out of his mind at worst. Jerry should have gotten someone for Joan weeks ago; she could have gotten hurt already. Thankfully, that hadn't happened and Carmen was on the job now.

After taking a few moments to recover from the ranting, she gathered up the papers and recipe cards to pocket them again. When she got home, she would have to call her friend from the police department and give him the letters. She hoped that Joan wasn't this stalker's first obsession and that he would fit the profile of a known criminal so he could get picked up and be off the streets.

Carmen was going to have to be extremely watchful tonight, but not be overly obvious about it. That was always a fine line to walk. If this guy was as dangerous as he had alluded to – or even half as irrational – she needed to make sure he didn't know that Joan hired herself a bodyguard. That would just aggravate the situation and could cause him to snap.

Joan stepped out around the time that she said she would. Her hair was done into a fishtail braid, and she wore a shirt ripped up all the way up the back over tight fitting, black leggings. Joan found Carmen in the living room in front of the TV.

"You ready to go?"

Carmen glanced up when Joan came back into the room. "You look really nice." Joan smiled at that.

CHAPTER SIX

The drive to Prestige was brief, but the time Joan and her company had to wait to get into the club was even shorter. The bouncer recognized her immediately and allowed her in before the others behind the burgundy, velvet rope. A lurid beat filled her head as people danced on the floor and drank at the bar.

Carmen was immediately reminded why she didn't like clubs while on the job – not that she had forgotten, of course. But walking into the packed place refreshed her memory more than she would have liked it to. She tended to avoid these places when not working, just because too many people made her antsy. She could brave the club for the sake of her job, though.

Dark eyes scanned the crowd, scrutinizing everyone to look for any sort of threats. There were no ultra polished knives in sight, nor was there anyone with a neon sign above their heads reading, "Stalker." Satisfied that no one posed an immediate threat to her charge, she relaxed – if only by a fraction of a percent.

Rory and Bruce had beat them there by half an hour. Rory hailed Joan over to their corner. When she got there, Bruce passed her an icy tumbler full of some unnamed liquid. Joan took a shot, but didn't offer Carmen any. If Carmen wanted to drink, she was welcome to have some so long as she could still drive legally at the end of the night.

"Where's Tony?" Joan asked.

Rory nodded out to the floor. "Picking up hotties, bastard."

Joan's eyes followed Rory's gaze to the drummer killing it on the dance floor with a pair of attractive ladies. Man, if he brought half of that energy to the stage her band would be set. Her haunted, blue stare left the sight of a few people enjoying themselves and drifted through the nightclub.

A man in a tie made Joan's heart stop. She leaned back until gravity required she step back to keep from falling over as the innocent man sipped his martini at the bar. Joan suddenly bumped into something- someone, and that finally got her heart going again.

"Sorry, Carmen." Joan glanced at the woman before looking back at the bar. It wasn't him. It wasn't Stan; it was just some guy in a fucking tie, for Christ's sake.

Strong hands went to Joan's shoulders, steadying the woman. "It's all right," Carmen said reassuringly. "Try and relax. I've got your back."

Joan chastised herself for panicking like that and pulled herself from Carmen's grip. She stood by the table and poured herself another shot; she wasn't going to relax without it, that was for sure.

A curious stare watched the singer with interest. Something was up and Rory knew it. With a shaky hand, Joan had just poured herself a double and the shot glass could barely hold it all. Rory stood up from his seat and waited for Joan to finish her shot before putting an arm around her shoulders and guiding her a couple feet away from her bodyguard.

"You all right, sweetheart?"

Joan tried to smile at her friend, but her grin cracked under the pressure of lying. "I just need to relax," she quoted Carmen.

After a moment's thought, Rory pulled a thin vial from one of his pockets and passed it to the singer. Joan took the white drug from his fingers without a word. It was cocaine – and half of the fun was the danger of addiction it promised.

64

"Tony needed help relaxing, too," Rory pointed out with a knowing smirk.

The lights flashed around the pair as the DJ switched tracks. A group of women screamed their approval for the song. Joan lived for that – for that energy and adoration. While her back was turned to most of the crowd, Joan opened the vial and held it up to her nose. She snorted the powder with one intake, as if she'd done it before.

Within the first few seconds, Joan's sinuses felt clear. The drug went right through the thin membrane of her nostrils to her bloodstream. She was hit with a wave of euphoria and brought an arm around Rory to squeeze him tight.

"Thanks, man." Smiling, Joan felt like she could do anything and nothing could stop her.

As for Stan the Stalker, fuck Stan the Stalker. He couldn't touch her, no one could. Joan was invincible tonight, and the dance floor was calling out her name.

A watchful eye stayed on Joan, even as she moved away from Carmen. Though the singer's back had been turned, Carmen saw something exchange hands and the way that Joan moved after that trade was a tell-tale sign of what had happened. Joan wasn't the first person that Carmen had babysat, who liked to use.

Ah, the beauty of discretion.

Carmen rubbed her left temple, closing her eyes for the barest of moments. Watching people get high was her favorite pastime- oh, wait. No, it wasn't.

She was tempted to grab Joan and drag her out kicking and screaming. Instead, she stayed where she was, making sure she maintained a good line of sight while trying to make it look like she wasn't observing Joan's every move. This wasn't what she thought she had signed up for, but there was fine print on every contract.

Joan stayed out on the floor dancing to song after song, track after track. If anyone recognized her, they also recognized that she was out to have a good time. She certainly wasn't the biggest celebrity in the club tonight and that played out in her favor. Joan fraternized with her bandmates and their company, they did shots and laughed.

This was the old life that the singer was missing out on ever since Stan had stepped out from the shadows. The snuff of cocaine gave her the confidence she needed to be herself again.

The time dragged by mercilessly for Carmen. She kept an eye on Joan and the rest of the crowd, but besides a lot of dancing and drinking, there wasn't much going on. She didn't impede on Joan's good time, she stayed back and let things transpire.

A couple of times she was approached by folks she had worked with before – famous folks, of course. They obviously wanted to know who she was working with now and why, but they got nothing out of her except for small talk. Once upon a time, the celebrities would have made her nervous, but after holding someone's hair while she hunkered over a toilet bowl, having to practically carry another to their limo, and keeping a guy from getting into a fist fight, that was all gone. She was growing tired of seeing famous people at their worst – and she'd only been doing this for eight months.

The club crowd was beginning to dwindle as people left to go home. Joan wasn't that tired, but she did remember that Carmen was tied to her as long as she was out. Wishing her boys a good night, Joan found Carmen nearby as 2 AM rolled around. Perhaps a little too boldly, Joan threaded her arm in Carmen's and beamed at the other woman.

66

"Shall we?"

Carmen tensed at the physical contact. "Yeah... let's go," she said with a nod, pulling her arm away from Joan's so she could lead the way out.

Joan hardly noticed the way Carmen reacquired her personal space. She merely acted as she should, following Carmen out of the club for the evening. She felt a little guilty for keeping the bodyguard out so late, but the egotistical part of her was telling herself that it was a part of Carmen's job and the woman knew what to expect.

Luckily for Carmen, Joan didn't normally go out on Saturdays. At least, not to party like this.

Carmen took Joan out to the SUV, making sure she got into the passenger's seat all right before going around and getting in the driver's seat. She started up the vehicle and drove away from the club like so many others were doing at the moment. The crowd had actually been quite tame compared to others she had seen. It tended to be at private events that celebrity-packed parties got out of hand.

"Jerry gave me your typical weekday schedule. Are you planning on going anywhere tomorrow?" she questioned as she drove them back to Joan's building.

"No, ma'am," Joan answered, as serious as she was drunk. She just thought it was so interesting that Carmen was a Marine. Joan couldn't imagine what that life was like, but she was dying to. It would probably be a good twenty minutes before they arrived at the penthouse.

She had to kill the time *somehow*. Being cooped up in the SUV was going to drive her up the wall, courtesy of the bound, vibrating nerves cocaine gave her.

"Have you ever killed anybody? I mean, Jesus-" Joan shook her head, trying to clear her thoughts. A little voice in the back of her head was telling her to shut up, but she wanted to know.

Carmen pursed her lips, gripping the steering wheel a little tighter. So much for a quiet drive. She was deathly silent for long moments, not even debating whether or not to answer, just trying to level her nerves to speak.

"We're not going to talk about it," she finally told Joan.

Carmen's total shut down felt like a thorn in Joan's side. The little voice got louder, proud of itself for being right and rubbing Joan's dry nose it in. It felt like the skin of her inner nostrils might crack and bleed, but Joan held it together.

"I'm sorry," she said quickly. "I didn't mean-" *Stop talking about this. Stop talking, just stop.* Joan rubbed her hands over her knees, pulling at the fabric of her jeans with cold fingers. *Stop, stop, stop.* She couldn't quit moving, but she did let them fall into silence. The sooner Joan was out of the SUV and got some fresh air, she would feel better.

Maybe she would head up to the balcony. Maybe she could stop moving, stop thinking up there.

Carmen pulled the SUV up in front of Joan's building after what felt like a gauntlet of stop lights and lane changes. "I'm going to walk you up, make sure you get inside okay," she told the singer before getting out of the car. She walked around to the passenger side and opened up the door for Joan.

As quietly as she could Joan got out of the car and walked with Carmen up to the Marmax building. This was one of those times she wished she didn't have to get into an elevator to get home, but even though she was pumped full of energy she wouldn't dare hit up the stairwell in high heels when there were twelve floors between herself and the penthouse.

Once inside, Joan's phone chimed, telling her

she had a new text message. She waited to check it until they were inside the elevator, thankful for something to do with her hands. The message was from Rory, asking if she'd gotten home all right. She sent a reply as the elevator moved.

Carmen stood to the side on the elevator, arms crossed over her chest. She had hoped Joan would be different from the rest, not binging on alcohol and drugs – but she supposed that was just the celebrity lifestyle. If given the chance, she would have stopped the rocker from using. She was here for the woman's well-being, not to be forced on the sidelines while Joan did whatever she wanted. Apparently the risks of addiction and the heightened probability of something bad happening while high didn't matter to Joan.

When the elevator finally stopped, Carmen stepped out first and walked to the singer's penthouse so she could open it up for the woman.

Being in the elevator was a strange sensation for Joan. Not only did she despise the enclosed space, but the fact that it was moving up without looking like it was moving made her dizzy. Booze wasn't helping that, neither was cocaine. So when the doors finally opened, Joan was right on Carmen's ass, anxious to be out of there.

Inside the penthouse was another story. Joan emptied her pockets, setting everything but her phone inside a crystal bowl on a counter. She knew she was about to be alone and that thought made her sadder than she was prepared to deal with. Her eyes watered and her nose burned as she turned to face away from Carmen and walked to her fish tank.

"Thanks for getting me home," Joan whispered. "I'll see you later." She pretended to fiddle with the equipment, as if she had to adjust the water temperature or something. She wanted to appear busy, to give reason for why she wouldn't look at Carmen.

Carmen sighed, seeing through the rocker's front. "You're a shit liar," she recounted her words from before. "Even when you're not trying to lie." She heard Joan's voice crack through her whispered words. Damn woman, tugging at her heart strings.

"Come on. What are you going to do now? Sit on the couch, balcony? Go to bed?" she questioned, shutting the front door and stepping further into the penthouse.

Joan didn't get it; she was sure Carmen was on her way out the door. Instead, Carmen was trying to wrangle her into calming down by spending time with her. As for Carmen's questions, there was no way Joan was ready to go to bed. The only reason she had left the club in the first place was so that her bodyguard could retire for the evening.

"You can go," Joan tried again. "Jerry's not paying you to watch me at my own place."

"He's paying me to watch out for your well-being," Carmen corrected. "And being drunk *and* high isn't very good for that." She walked over to Joan, gently taking her by the arm and guiding her over toward the balcony. "Oh, and by the way, if I see coke in your hand again, there's going to be hell to pay. Your buddy is going to be lucky if he doesn't get his ass kicked." She took Joan outside, knowing the fresh air would be good for her. "Have a seat, I'm going to get you some water."

Already being inebriated, Carmen's threat didn't do much for Joan. She was just surprised that the bodyguard knew about the cocaine. What was Carmen expecting? That a rocker wouldn't do drugs? That was like a church without an altar, or an ocean without beaches.

Thinking of those calm waters, Joan

approached the balcony. She took off her high heels and then rested her elbows on the smooth metal railing. The sounds of passing cars and groups of bar-goers walking home filtered up from below. San Diego was just as bright as it had been hours ago, when the night life was fully pumping through the city's veins. In a couple of hours, the sun would rise behind her, but this was Joan's favorite time of night.

All the people in the service industry, the blue-collar workers, and the 9-5'ers were asleep in their beds. Meanwhile, young adults were drinking and fucking until their problems disappeared into an afterthought. Joan was still jaded over how the world worked. She was just like them, angry and sad – and wondering how people went on in a place like this. And why.

Joan looked down over the balcony, incipient thoughts poisoning her overactive mind. She courted the ledge like beautiful, unhappy women tended to do, but she wasn't on her way over. She hadn't hit that low, or that kind of high.

Carmen went to the kitchen and got a glass of ice water, hoping it would help her charge. If there was one part of her job that she hated most, it was picking up the pieces after a binge. These were grown adults, she wasn't an adult-sitter – honestly, sometimes she wished candy bribes would get these people into bed. This was turning into one of those nights.

There were days when it was hard not to be filled with contempt for her job or the people she worked for. Somehow lots of money and fame turned into drug and alcohol abuse, and in the worst cases it resulted in death. How could these people be so angry with the world when they hadn't actually seen the worst of it?

Glass of water and a couple of aspirin in her possession, she walked back out to the balcony. "Here,

71

chica," she said as she walked over to Joan. "You're going to want this."

Joan took the medication in one hand and the drink with another. She did as Carmen bid her, more in the mood to wrestle than argue. She had been on a slow decline since they left the club as her intoxication wore off. While she had no dinner that night, she wasn't hungry. If there was a secret weight loss program in Cali – it was doing coke, lots of it. The drug suppressed appetite like nothing else.

Carmen looked out at the city while Joan did as she was told. Despite her frustration, she still had a job to do. Maybe when she called her buddy, she'd see if he could get her out of this line of business. Eight months was enough, and she was tired of watching people destroy themselves.

When half the glass was empty, Joan set it on the ground next to her shoes. A plane flew overhead, drowning out all other noise for a few seconds. In that time, Joan decided she was going to tell Carmen something she should have told her earlier.

"He always wears a red tie when I see him. He always dresses like... he works on Wall Street or he's about to go on a date. He's white, probably almost six foot," she finished. She didn't know what other information she could give Carmen about his physical appearance.

At first when Joan spoke, Carmen couldn't figure out what she was talking about. Then she realized it was an account – of the stalker.

"Okay, that's good. I can work with that," she said with a nod. Even if it was a pretty generic description, she had something to look for now. Joan absorbed some of the praise, letting it filter through the remnants of her high.

Carmen turned around and leaned back against the retaining wall of the balcony, resting her

72

elbows on it. She saw how hard it was for Joan to speak on the subject and figured it would show a bit of solidarity if she offered up a bit about her own life.

"The answer to your question earlier... is yes."

Joan grit her teeth. So, Carmen was a killer; she never should have asked.

"I'm sorry," she said, looking across her shoulder to see if Carmen would meet her gaze. "I didn't mean to pry."

Carmen kept staring straight ahead, her interest falling to the door that lead back into the penthouse. She couldn't bring herself to look over at Joan after the revelation. Though it had been years since she was on active duty, it was still something she didn't like to talk about. Even though women weren't sent to fight in the beginning, it was hard to tell when an ambush was coming – and in a war, live combat was hard to avoid.

"It's okay," she told Joan. "You have a right to know about the person that's keeping you safe."

Joan sighed and looked away. Tonight was turning out to be a pretty big mistake as far as Carmen went. Joan shouldn't have called Jerry about the stalker. He hadn't shown himself since that night and he never did anything to make her think he could be dangerous. Stan was just a little funny in the head; he was just shy.

"You can crash in the guest room if you don't want to drive home right now." Joan stood up from her leaning position to head inside. She wasn't very tired but she could lay down for a while. The guest room was fully made up; both Rory and Bruce had stayed there before after more than one wild night.

Carmen followed her charge back into the penthouse. If she didn't have work to do for Joan's case, she probably would have stayed the night just to keep an eye on the woman. Booze and drugs could be harsh on their own, and together they just compounded each other. But there was a very real threat to Joan's life, and she had to take it seriously.

"Actually, I've got a meeting in about four hours," she said after checking her watch, seeing that it was just after three. They were both night owls, and he could help her with this case. "So, if you think you'll be all right, I'll head home. You can call me if you need anything, or if you decide you want to go somewhere tomorrow."

"All right," Joan said, running her fingers to the end of her braid to undo the tie. With the band around her wrist she shook out the lower half of her braid, blonde hair falling in light curls at her shoulder. She would get ready for bed but there was no telling if she would sleep. She usually didn't – on the nights she snorted coke. Maybe she would sit down in a shirt and panties, and bust out her guitar while she fucked around with some lyrics that had been dodging her conscious mind between thoughts.

"Good night, Carmen."

"Take it easy tonight, okay, Joan?" Carmen asked. "I'll have my phone on me, even in the meeting, so call if you need anything." She headed for the door, stopping as she placed her hand on the brass knob. "Good night."

After that, she stepped out of the expensive apartment, and made sure to lock the door behind herself – just in case the action slipped past Joan's memory. She took the elevator down to the first floor and headed out of the building. Her phone was in her hand before she got to her SUV, and she pulled up a familiar name. As she opened her door and got in, she hit the 'call' button.

Half a beat after the first ring, the other end picked up. "Macrae," a deep, male voice answered.

"Hey Sam, it's Carmen," she said. "I've got a

new case that I need some help with. You busy?"

"For you, I'm never busy," he answered – Carmen could hear the smile in his voice. "You want to swing by, or should I come over to your place?"

"I just left my client's penthouse, so I'll come to you. Be there soon," she told him.

"All right, see you soon, Savedra," he replied before hanging up.

CHAPTER SEVEN

Carmen tossed her phone into the passenger seat and pulled away from the building. She decided to stop at one of the many still open drive-thrus and got herself and Sam a coffee before heading to the man's house.

With two cups of coffee in hand, she got out of the SUV and walked up to the moderate sized home. On the first floor, only two lights were still on; the second floor was completely dark. Before she got all the way up to the door, it opened and revealed her military buddy turned police officer.

Two massive pit bulls with sleepy eyes rushed out to greet her, tails wagging as they vied for Carmen's attention. "Hey, boys," she said with a chuckle. The dogs were beautiful – one was blue and the other had a spectacular brindle coat. They served as emotional support animals for the guy she was coming to see.

"Hey, Carmen," he greeted with a smile. Carmen remembered when the large, black man intimidated her. He yelled orders, never smiled, and he was so strict that his own damn shoelaces wouldn't dream of coming untied on their own. He had hair, then, too. Over their years in the Corps together, he had lightened up. Now, though, his grin was wide and he seemed genuinely happy.

"Staff Sergeant," Carmen replied, offering him one of the drinks.

"At ease, Corporal," he joked as he took the cup. "So, what have you got?" He closed the door after she was inside and led the way into his home office.

"I'm working with Joan Devintia. She's got

one hell of a stalker. This is something I'd expect to see from someone who's been in the spotlight for years... not just new like she is," Carmen explained as she sat down in front of his desk. She set her coffee down and pulled the letters out of her pocket. "Already opened. Her manager and I have both read them. He said he had someone in Forensics run them for prints, nothing came back. When more come in, he's going to give them straight to me."

Sam nodded as he listened, reaching across the desk for the small stack of papers and recipe cards. He started looking the letters over, brow furrowing deeply.

"No name or alias, no return address... but what's with the recipe cards?"

"I don't know, but I'll probably never eat cheesecake again." Carmen shuddered. "Same fluted handwriting with each letter. Obviously, it's the same guy writing it. Joan finally gave me a description of him this evening – nothing remarkable except that he's always in a suit and tie."

"Even that's not very remarkable," Sam pointed out. He frowned as he skimmed through the short letters, now seeing exactly what his friend was talking about. "Shit. This guy is... grade-A insane."

"Joan doesn't know about these. We need to keep it that way, if we can. She's a lot more delicate than she lets on. She's got a pretty good front put up."

"Careful, Savedra. I might actually think you care about someone."

"Oh, shut up." Carmen rolled her eyes. "Not all of us can live the American dream with the house, white picket fence, trophy wife, two-point-five kids..."

"We don't have two-point-five kids, we have three full ones," Sam replied.

"Oh, excuse me, my mistake. But you know what? I think I'm ready to settle down for my own piece of the American dream. That offer to get me on the force still stand?"

"Of course it does, but I'm surprised you'd give this up. What you're doing... we can't do as police. We have to wait until something happens, and we can't always be right there next to the people who need help."

"I think this one is it for me, Sam," Carmen shook her head. "I'm tired of watching people our age and younger destroy themselves."

"You think the P.D. is any different? I think it's probably worse, and for less money. I only make a decent paycheck because of my rank in the military and my uncle."

"I've got a decent savings account still," Carmen pointed out. "Any kind of income will work. I may as well feel like I'm doing something good... like I have a purpose beyond sitting on the sidelines and watching people snort coke and get drunk off their asses." She took another drink of her coffee, relaxing back into her chair.

"Well, at least you don't have a wife and kids to support," Sam nodded. He finished flipping through the notes, and then placed them on the desk. "I'll have to check our database to see if this guy lines up with any known criminals, and I can see what a forensic linguist says. It might take some time." He turned to his computer, punching in his password and pulling up the database. He entered the physical search criteria that Carmen gave him, then started comparing what he had from the letters to what was on file.

Carmen waited patiently, glad for the man's help. He had been the Staff Sergeant of her squad in the Marines. They had seen a lot together – their whole squad had seen more than anyone should have in the time they spent together. They went through hell and high water to get their missions accomplished, then turned around and stormed right back into it again.

"So," she began speaking some time later, "this guy says he's armed. He's threatened Joan's life. I haven't had anything quite like this – just the run of the mill, creepy dude who hangs around too often. Where do I fall, legally?"

Sam stopped what he was doing and folded his hands in front of himself. "You can detain him, if you're sure it's him and he comes anywhere near your client. If we had a name, we could issue a cease and desist, and a restraining order on him. Since we don't, there's not much I can do from here. If he decides to become a threat to your client's life and attempts an attack, do what they tell us – use the minimum amount of force necessary to regain control of the situation. You've got your concealed carry and private officer licenses?"

"Of course."

"Good. Make sure you've got all your t's crossed and i's dotted with those, because it may come down to using your weapon. Make sure they're up to date; make sure your weapon is registered."

Carmen nodded as she listened to him. She hoped it wouldn't come down to having to use her gun, but if it did, she was well aware of what would happen afterward. It wasn't like what Hollywood made people think. You couldn't just drop your weapon and have everything be fine. Being an active shooter, you would be arrested and held overnight while the preliminary investigation was done.

"I'll make sure my information is all current with the P.D. and Sheriff's office," she assured him. "Anything come up on your database?"

Sam shook his head. "I'm sorry, Carmen. It didn't. I'm making a new case file. I need to keep these letters for evidence. Your guy's description will be in the system now. If you can get any more on him let me know, and I'll get it updated." He punched a few keys, always needing to look at where his fingers were placed, but then he paused. "You know, if your client is the new kid on the block, maybe her case is more like what we see every day."

"What do you mean?" Carmen perked up in her chair.

"Three out of four victims know their stalker in some capacity. Hell, from what I've seen, it's usually the ex-boyfriend, but it could be anyone she's had contact with. Someone in her neighborhood, someone she works with. It could be the pizza guy."

Carmen scoffed. "Way to make me paranoid."

"Use your common sense, and you'll be fine."

More tense than she was before, Carmen got to her feet. "All right, thanks for the help, man. I owe you one."

"No... I don't think you do. I've still got quite a bit to repay you for," Sam replied. He pushed out his chair and walked Carmen to the door. "Be careful with this guy. Don't underestimate him."

"Look at you, getting all worried about me," she teased, pushing his shoulder. "Don't worry. If I can take you down in a sparring match, this asshole won't be a problem."

"You *used* to be able to. I don't think you could now," he replied with a smirk. Sam opened up the door and let the woman out of the house.

"Yeah, yeah. Try and save your pride. Tell Maria and the kids I said 'Hi.' I'll call you if anything else comes up." Carmen turned and walked down the sidewalk back to her SUV. The sun was already up over the horizon – she didn't realize she'd spent so much time at the house. It was definitely time to catch some sleep.

~*~

The basement dwelling where he lived was lit by a single light bulb hanging overhead. Furnishings were sparse – the only Earthly possession he needed was still just outside his grasp. Pictures of his idol – his *angel* – were littered everywhere: taped to the walls, laying on his desk, spread across the single bed. He could see her everywhere he looked.

"So beautiful," he whispered, fingers running across one of the magazine clippings taped on his wall.

He sat down at his desk, a black marker and a very particular piece of paper laid out before him. He reached into the top drawer and pulled on a pair of latex gloves, eyes fixed on yet another picture of Joan Devintia. After they were on, he slowly pulled his gaze away from that angelic face and looked down at the laminated menu from The Orchid. He picked up his marker and delicately set the felt tip between appetizers.

"Dearest," he spoke allowed as he wrote. "You shouldn't let Rory talk you into such nasty habits. Your body is a temple – it's *my* temple. If you continue to desecrate that temple, I'll have no choice but to destroy it. Take better care of yourself, my angel, so when the time comes I can worship you properly."

It had been almost a fluke that he saw Joan going to Prestige, but he quickly followed. He saw everything that happened inside the club, from the cocaine to the rocker leaving with some woman. He gave her the benefit of the doubt, obviously Joan just worked with the stranger.

His angel wouldn't hurt him like that.

But how could she treat herself so recklessly? Surely she had to know he wouldn't approve of such behavior. Of course she knew.

She did it to spite him.

The world hounded him with a sudden blow to his sense of balance. Pain stabbed at the front of and top of his head. He lifted both hands, clutching his forehead and panting heavily. Breathing in the marker fumes made his stomach roll. He groaned unhappily, grabbing the front of the desk to anchor himself.

Minutes ticked past before the pain subsided and the world stilled. He grabbed the dagger that was laying on the desk, turned and plunged the blade into the wall beside him – directly through a picture of Joan.

"You bitch! Whore! How could you do that? How could you let other people touch you? You're mine!" he spat furiously. *"I'll gut you like a pig! How would you like that, hm? You let everyone around you treat you like a piece of meat! I'll make sure you end up like one!"*

He pulled his hand away from the handle of the dagger, getting up to vent his anger. He ripped the latex gloves off and threw them across the room, pacing. How could she do this to him? She knew he was there; knew he was watching. Yet everything she had done, was done to make him angry with her.

"You're making a fool of me!" he roared as he spun to face the offending picture again.

Just like the flip of a switch, his mood changed. "Oh... Oh, Joan... I'm so sorry," he said apologetically as he rushed over to the wall. He quickly pulled the dagger out of the wall and handled the torn picture with the utmost care.

"My angel, I'm so sorry," he whispered, tears running freely down his cheeks. "It's okay, my sweet. It's okay. It won't happen again, I promise. You just... You just can't make me angry like that." His fingers traced the lines of her face as he composed himself again.

82

"I forgive you, Joan. It's all right," he told the picture reassuringly.

To calm down, he walked over to a small stereo system that was practically buried in jewel cases. Compulsively, he bought Joan's EP every time he saw one – multiple copies if he could. Each concert he went to, he made a recording and turned it into a bootleg CD. He opened the disc tray and switched out CDs.

"I love listening to you."

Joan's voice came to him like a soothing wave, but she wasn't singing.

"-place is… interesting."

Another voice cut in, still feminine but harder. It was Tanya Raine, Joan's mentor. This particular recording wasn't from a concert.

"You have to ignore the décor. I admit it's way too fancy for me. I mean- look at the waiters. Ties, really? But the food is amazing. They've got a great team of chefs on the weekends."

"Good thing it's Saturday," Joan agreed. Noise from a restaurant filtered in as plates were collected and conversations were held beyond the one between the pair of musicians. Joan cleared her throat before she spoke again. *"You know… I'm going to be sad when this is over."*

"Don't be! You've got so much to look forward to."

"Yeah, you're right. Hey, it's Rory's birthday. Help me embarrass him when he gets back and sing Happy Birthday with me."

"Am I getting paid for this?"

"That's what I asked Jerry before I agreed to tour with you," Joan teased. Both of the women shared a laugh, interrupted by static, and then Joan quieted them down. *"Oh! Here he comes."*

CHAPTER EIGHT

It was four in the afternoon the next day by the time Joan registered any kind of conscious thought that wasn't addled by her indulgences the night before. She had only fallen asleep for a few minutes, and she woke to the feeling of someone standing over her as they held her down by the shoulders. It was so disturbing she couldn't rest again.

Her phone rang, so she went to the counter to retrieve it. For a split second, as she read the caller ID, her eyebrows furrowed together. The number was unknown. Her somber ring tone only sounded for a moment more before the call suddenly ended. Joan hadn't even had a chance to think about answering it, let alone swipe a finger across the screen to do so.

"Huh."

She moved to put the iPhone down when it screamed for her attention again. Joan was so startled she almost dropped the device.

"Shit," she whispered, bringing the screen up to her face. The caller ID read: Hector R. The singer took a deep breath before she answered.

"Hello?"

"Joan, baby. Hey, how are you?"

A smile broke onto her face as she caught up with an old friend. The small talk was pleasant and pleasantly short. Hector got to the point quickly.

"I had a band cancel on me tonight," he informed her. "I was wondering if you'd come in, you know? I've been meaning to try and book you. Just play a few songs. You don't even have to do a full set, just gimme something to entertain the guys for- thirty minutes..." Hector was practically begging, Joan could tell.

"Well, you know I'm legit now," she responded, starting to pace through her apartment. "I can't say yes to you. You have to go through Jerry."

"I know, I know. I just thought if I buttered you up first... What with you becoming this big star overnight..."

"Oh, keep going."

"Uh... well, you're so pretty."

Joan chuckled. "Enough, enough. That was painful." She wanted to help her old friend. It would be nice to perform in her old haunt, but when profit was involved she was legally bound to perform only when her manager said it was all right. Had it been some kind of charity event or a small gathering of friends, that would have been different.

"Don't worry, I'll call him. I can spin it," Hector promised. "Think of it as a good time to promote your new CD. See you later, Joan."

"Yeah, bye." Joan shook her head when she got off the phone. She didn't doubt Hector's ability to convince Jerry into letting her go. Her former boss of sorts was right. Joan could promote her new music by playing a few songs of the old stuff. The bar crowd would love it because half of the regulars had been around when she was just starting to play. They knew her before she really got any air under her wings; they loved her first and she loved them for it.

It had been too long since she had stepped into the dimly lit, smoky atmosphere of Dodger's.

Carmen got home around eight o'clock that morning. She showered and had some breakfast before laying down on the couch. She certainly hadn't expected to pull an all-nighter, but that came with the territory sometimes. With some rerun of an old 90s show on the TV, she started to doze off. Her phone and gun were both within arm's reach.

It was hard to tell how long she'd been asleep when she jerked awake, her phone blaring away beside her. Having fallen asleep somewhere she wasn't used to, with so much noise around her, she automatically went into defensive mode. Her pistol was up and she was scanning the room before her consciousness caught up with her. It finally registered that she was home and her phone was ringing.

Heaving out a sigh, she reached out and grabbed the offending object. "Savedra," she answered.

"Ms. Savedra, this is Jerry Stevenson. Sorry to bother you on the weekend, but I've just had someone book Joan for a small gig," the man on the other line explained.

Setting her handgun down, Carmen sat up and rubbed her tired eyes. "All right. When and where?" she asked.

"Be there by 10 o'clock tonight, she'll play at 10:30," Jerry answered. "You'll be going to Dodger's. She'll play a few songs, so you should be out of there by 11:30."

"Yeah, yeah. All right," the Latina said. "We'll be there." She hung up the phone and set it down, running both hands over her face. It was jarring, to wake up in the state she did. If her working hours weren't so sporadic, she would have a dog like Sam did – but it was just so hard to take care of an animal when you didn't know when you'd be home, or how long you would be out at a time.

After several moments, she grabbed her phone to text Joan: *Jerry just called. I'll pick you up at 9:30.*

Sorry to bug you so soon after last night. If it wasn't for a friend, I would have declined.

Joan sent the return text before realizing that she needed to decide on a set list. Jerry gave her the go ahead to choose whatever she wanted to play since she would be going it alone with her guitar. That meant everything would be acoustic and she couldn't pick anything where the brothers' background vocals were very important. After a few minutes of internal debate, she decided on a few songs.

At Dodger's, she mostly played other people's music. If the crowd got it in their head to make a request like the old days, she would probably just have to oblige. She was a performer after all.

Carmen got ready to leave at 9 o'clock. Before hitting the door, she touched each one of the pockets of her cargo pants to make sure she had everything: gun in holster, handcuffs in nylon case, wallet, and keys. Satisfied that nothing would be left behind, she stepped out of her apartment and went down the single flight of stairs to the first floor. As she had told Joan, at 9:30 she knocked on the door to the rocker's penthouse before letting herself inside.

For once, Joan made sure she was totally ready to go before she had to leave. She was wearing leather, lots of leather, and plenty of jewelry, but it was a good look for her. She picked up her guitar case, painfully aware that the bodyguard hadn't even acknowledged her texted apology.

"Hey," she rasped.

"Hey," Carmen replied, holding the door open so that Joan could get out with her instrument. "How are you feeling?" Joan had to be functioning somewhat decently to agree to play a gig that night. It probably wasn't because she needed the money. For someone just coming onto the scene, Joan was doing well thanks to Jerry's management and the fact that she started this game debt free.

"I'm fine," Joan shrugged off Carmen's concern, not because she was ungrateful, but because she was used to the day-after crud. Coke was more of a once a week thing for her. She just used on the weekends that she partied. She could stop whenever she wanted.

Instead of setting her guitar down in the elevator, Joan held onto it for the entire ride. "Did you sleep?" she asked, timidly.

Carmen glanced over when Joan questioned her, offering a shrug. "A few hours," she answered. "You?" She knew that she'd told Joan to take it easy after she left, but that definitely didn't mean Joan would listen to her. Most of the time her advice fell on inattentive ears.

Joan knew she couldn't lie, so she didn't try. She shook her head as they reached the ground floor. Joan let Carmen lead the way out to her SUV and loaded her guitar in the back. Cocaine was an energizer; it didn't allow for rest. Joan's nightmares weren't too keen on letting her sleep either.

Once the two of them were settled into the vehicle, Carmen started it and pulled away from the building. "I'm glad you told me about him last night," Denial and avoidance were always so much easier than taking a problem head on. "I know it had to be hard for you."

Had Joan done that? It took her a moment to register the fact that she did indeed tell Carmen about her stalker.

"Yeah, sure," she replied, a little despondent. She had also been a royal bitch and cornered the other woman into talking about something that was none of Joan's business. Her conviction had faltered since then. Despite the still uneasy feeling in her gut, she was beginning to wonder if having a bodyguard was necessary. Nothing had happened since the night at The Orchid.

Carmen quirked a brow at the callous response. She let it slide, though. If Joan didn't want to talk, that was fine by her. She wouldn't make an attempt at it again. Maybe it was better that way.

Carmen got them to the bar on time and stayed by Joan's side once they got out of the vehicle. She walked inside with Joan, hoping that this outing wouldn't be nearly as long or drug and booze filled as their last.

Hector met Joan at the door with his usual boisterous nature. Joan hadn't seen him in months, but he was still as funny as ever. After quick pleasantries and a brief hug was shared with the Hawaiian, Joan motioned to Carmen and made sure Hector was aware that Carmen wasn't just some bar-crawler. Whether or not Hector assumed Carmen was a personal assistant, that was his prerogative. He could think Carmen was her dealer for all she really cared so long as the other woman was treated with same respect that Joan got.

As a part of the contract, Hector was obliged to introduce Joan before she took to the small stage inside Dodger's. No one heckled Joan for autographs before the show, but she got to talk to her fair share of friendly patrons. This place was her paycheck before she got her big break; it was practically her home – Hector a loving brother willing to give Joan a microphone and a loan for a guitar. So long as she continued to keep people entertained while they drank the bar out of beer.

It was here that she made enough money to keep the lights on in her apartment so she could stay up all night after a shift and write original music. It was this place that gave her a chance, and she wasn't going to waste it. Joan felt sentimental as she looked across the stage at her old, worn barstool and that familiar – if not a bit faulty – mic.

"Ladies and gentlemen. Oh, who am I kidding?" Hector raddled the small crowd. "We all know there aren't any ladies here!" Some women cheered as guys whistled, hoisting their drinks in the air. "I've finally convinced a familiar face to get her ass out of that high-rise penthouse before she gets too comfortable." Joan shook her head as some voices jeered and guffawed at her. Hector smiled as he leaned down to speak in the microphone. "Give it up for Joan Devintia!" The man held out his hand in her direction, willing her to take the stage as the crowd obliged his request. The regular bar-goers were ravenous for Joan, feeling a little nostalgic themselves.

Joan stepped onto the stage, guitar in hand. It was hard to see out into Dodger's, what with Hector's bright-as-the-sun, hundred-dollar spotlight pointed right her. But Joan didn't need to see the people to know how they were feeling. The energy of the place was rowdy, but good. After a few brief words with the crowd, and one humorous exchange with an old drunk, Joan found her seat and set the guitar in her lap.

She didn't know where Carmen was, but she was sure that Carmen was watching her. Everyone was; she could feel their eyes like threads from a spiderweb that she had walked right into the second she put one boot onto the platform.

Carmen settled herself at an empty table up next to the stage. She sat on the side of it, giving herself a great view of the performance area and the rest of the bar. She couldn't see any of these patrons making a problem for her charge. It was obvious they loved Joan and were happy to see her back in their midst. Going out this time was going to be much tamer than last night.

As Joan started to play and sing, one of the waitresses came by the table and set a drink in front of Carmen. "What's this?" she asked, looking up at a redhead with a brilliant smile.

90

"On the house," the woman answered. "You looked like you could use a drink."

"Thank you, but I'm on the clock," Carmen replied. "I can't drink any booze tonight."

The redhead pouted a bit, picking the drink back up. "Is there something else I can get you, sweetheart?"

"Well... since it's on the house and you asked so nice," Carmen began with a smirk. "How about a Jack and Coke, minus the Jack?"

The server's smile returned just like that. "You got it." She turned and went back to the bar quickly to get the drink.

While she waited, Carmen's attention returned to the stage. A few moments later, the waitress returned. Carmen took the drink with a grateful nod and didn't miss the ten numbers written on the coaster that came with it.

"Thank you," she said. There was a time she would have called the number with too much confidence; there was a time she didn't even have enough confidence to consider it. And then there was tonight, when she was flattered but still afraid.

"You're welcome," the waitress replied. "You should call me when you're not on the clock."

Carmen's stomach dropped. "I would, but I'm seeing someone." She could manage a lie, unlike Joan. What she couldn't handle was direct eye contact. She looked off, brown eyes naturally going straight to her charge.

"Oh, shit." The waitress laughed at herself. "I'm sorry. I did *not* realize you were with Joan-"

Carmen was in the middle of taking a drink when she tried to kill the assumption. "I... I, what?"

"-That's great. She deserves someone who makes her happy."

Too busy trying not to cough and interrupt Joan's husky vocals, Carmen couldn't get a response out before the server was gone. Half of her soda vanished before the itch left the back of her throat. The thought of dating Joan was still lodged in her mind though, right next to Joan's hypnotic chord progression.

Joan did her set; three songs from her EP played out just like they were supposed to be. People were happy with her acoustic performance, too happy Joan decided. Between bouts of loud clapping a chant grew from the bar.

"Encore! Encore! Encore!"

The rocker bit her lip and adjusted herself on the seat. She really hadn't planned to go on. A lot of stuff that was happening lately, she hadn't planned on. But the group wanted what they wanted, and Joan wasn't going to deny them. She settled on one more song; something that would fit the rest of her blood-pumping, beer-drinking, angry set list. She put her fingers in place, counting down in her head-

"Play something new!"

Joan heard the cry right as the crowd died down, ready for her next song. Tilting her head for a moment, she spoke into the microphone. "Something new, huh? All right. This is from my first album, *Snowball Earth*," she told them. "No one else has heard this song, so you drunk bastards better buy the CD." After a few hearty laughs, the bar patrons got quiet again. Joan knew what song she should play. "Volcano" would have been perfect here. It was the first single from her album and Jerry thought it had real potential, but acoustically... Joan knew what song would sound the best.

Carmen had actually listened to the music this time around. A few songs weren't bad to sit through, but suddenly the crowd wanted more. The next song...

92

Carmen knew exactly what it was about as soon as the woman started. She placed both arms on the table in front of her as Joan's emotionally-charged voice took precedence over anything else.

"I'll be so dangerous to you."

Joan picked up the tune with her guitar. She could tell she had the audience's full attention by their silence.

"Haunt you and slip right through
Your defenses
They will not save you
Baby, I'm going to find you
And I'm going to maim you."

With an electric guitar, it was quite the power ballad. Alone, with just her voice and her solitary instrument, it was as evocative as Joan meant it to be.

"Ready, set, start
Cut to the chase
My favorite part
Ready, set, start
Cut to the chase
My favorite part."

If any musician ever said their work wasn't from personal experience, they were liars or frauds. That much – Joan knew for a fact. She poured all of her fear into this song, every ounce of nightmare and increment of terror. Joan was a hunted woman, and this song was proof enough of how she really felt about it. As much as she wanted to deny that she needed Carmen to protect her, her music laid her bare for the world to see.

"Oh, what it takes out of me
To hunt you down, so patiently
You opened the door
You uncaged the beast
And this monster wants its whore."

"Ready, set, start
Cut to the chase
My favorite part."

People weren't so quick to ask for more music this time. They seemed a little shell-shocked, until a woman sitting in the back got to her feet and cheered.

"Damn, girl!"

Applause broke out again, but Joan couldn't bring herself to smile or lounge around. She said a fast, tame thank you and walked away.

When Joan left the stage, Carmen was up and at her side in bare seconds. Obviously, she'd been right about Joan when talking to Sam: the woman was more delicate than she let on. It was a good thing that she hadn't seen those letters.

How did Joan keep forgetting there was someone out there, watching her back? How did she keep forgetting about Carmen? Because suddenly, Carmen was standing right in front of her and Joan hadn't been expecting it. The woman's jaw twitched as she stopped in her tracks to keep from running Carmen over.

Joan didn't waste time with small talk. "Let's go." Hector got what he wanted, Jerry was already paid, and she was in no mood for any familiar friends to ask what in God's name that last song was about.

"Okay," Carmen said with a nod, a sympathetic look in her eyes. She guided Joan out of the bar, acting as a buffer for the singer as they left. Anyone who wanted to stop and talk was immediately shut down. She got Joan out of the bar quickly and headed to the SUV.

"Take a breath, you're okay," she assured Joan. It didn't take a rocket scientist to figure out what had the woman spooked, so Carmen tried to ground her again.

94

Joan was too tired to fuss. After she placed her guitar in the back, she fell against the SUV. Leaning her head back against the metal frame, Joan closed her eyes – fighting off her one real monster. A stalker she named Stan.

"Do you get paid extra for all the emotional support?" she joked. Her lungs were a bit short on air, so the statement was half of a question and half of a gasp for more oxygen. "I hope you do."

Carmen stayed right next to Joan as the singer leaned back against her vehicle. Once upon a time she'd fought off demons in the same manner. Hell, just a couple years ago – she wouldn't have been able to be in such a tight space with so many people. She'd come a long way. Carmen still had some things that wouldn't go away, but she adapted.

"No," she answered with a smile. "I actually don't." She lifted a hand, hesitating slightly before closing the distance between it and Joan's shoulder. Carmen wasn't a big fan of being touched – and God help the person who touched her when she wasn't expecting it. But she remembered it was a human thing to do, and it was supposed to be comforting. "It's just a little something extra I throw in."

Joan felt a fire stir within her, hotter than twenty of Hector's hundred-dollar spotlights. It flashed across her skin, starting from the place where Carmen touched her. The woman bolstered a fake grin before breathing got too difficult. Even though they were out in the open with the cool autumn air, Joan could feel space closing in around her.

She anchored herself, placing a shaky hand on top of Carmen's. "I think- I'm... having a panic attack..." Joan shook her head, willing the anxiety away. Her lungs were straining and her knees were locking up. This wasn't good; this was different than the fear she was used to.

"Okay, it's all right," Carmen told her. "Come here. I want you to sit down." She was careful not to crowd Joan as she opened the back end of the SUV again and had her sit down. It was the most open space she could offer for Joan to sit at the moment.

"Take long, deep inhales through your mouth, hold it, then exhale through your nose," she instructed Joan. There was a kit stashed in the back of the SUV for just such an occasion since Carmen was no stranger to such attacks. She stepped to the side and reached further into the back end, grabbing a red case out from under the back seat. She undid the clips and opened it up, revealing three bottles of water, individually wrapped straws, a stress ball, and a few individual packets of oyster crackers next to first aid supplies.

Carmen grabbed a bottle of water and opened it up. She then got a straw and unwrapped it, dropping it into the drink before offering the bottle to Joan.

"Sip slowly. Don't take full drinks."

Joan heard Carmen speak, but if felt like several long seconds had passed before she followed the directions. It was a constant battle, reminding herself that she was safe – that there was no need to panic here.

The cool water was a blessing, but it was hard not to choke on. Which was probably why Carmen had said to drink it *slowly*. Joan began to calm down. If the press got wind of this, some hardcore bitch she would turn out to be. *Joan Devintia has panic attack outside local bar. Fans, not impressed.* The vain woman could have laughed at herself – well, she could have if she was able to breathe, and that was still giving her trouble.

Joan set the bottle down, careful not to spill it in the back of Carmen's SUV. Her attention was diverted away from herself and to the fact that

Carmen had pulled out what was essentially some kind of emergency kit for this kind of situation. Why did Carmen have it all ready to go? Did the bodyguard need it for herself? PTSD was a potent side-effect of military service in a time of war, and lately, the US was always at war. Joan's heart ached, still in pain from the attack, but there was something more to it. Joan hurt for the Marine, whose prepared mind had made this kit a necessity to have with her wherever she went.

Carmen stood by the SUV, close enough to offer Joan the comfort of security, but far enough that she wouldn't feel like she was being surrounded. She knew how it felt to have the world closing in around you – it wasn't fun. At least Joan had someone who knew how to deal with anxiety attacks, and not someone who would just make it worse by saying something like, "Just get over it."

Slowly, Carmen turned and grabbed one of the individual packs of oyster crackers. She opened it up and offered it to Joan.

"One at a time. Don't chew, let them dissolve."

Joan took the offered miniature snack. This would be the first thing she ate since lunch yesterday, and it was oyster crackers... She placed one in her mouth, continuing to breathe through her nose, and swallowed when it dissolved. A couple more crackers later, she found she could speak again and glanced at the kit.

"You've done this-" Joan glanced at the kit, "before, haven't you?" She wasn't trying to be nosey, and she was pretty sure she already knew the answer to her question, but she really did want to know more about Carmen.

"Wouldn't keep it in my car if I didn't," Carmen pointed out. She was glad to see that Joan seemed to be calming back down. "Feeling better?"

Joan nodded and set the half-empty packets of crackers down. The water helped her cool down and the mild snack gave her something else to focus on.

"Yeah, I am." The physical collapse of her usually involuntary functions, left for a weakness in her mental fortitude. "I hate music sometimes," she whispered, trying to give Carmen a little insight as to why she had freaked out like she did. "I love it, but I hate it."

"I can see why," Carmen responded. She closed up the kit and put it back where it was before sitting down with Joan. She didn't sit too closely to the rocker, not wanting to start the attack all over again. "But, as long as I'm around, you're safe until we catch this guy. I promise. And you're not alone, either."

Those words helped Joan almost as much as Carmen's knowledge on how to handle the situation. In fact, it might have helped more. The ache in her chest dissipated with every word. Joan set her hands down on either side of her, not realizing how close she was to Carmen until the back of her hand brushed against the other woman's leg. Carmen had tried to keep space between them, but the back of an SUV only allowed for so much.

She would have pulled her hand back and apologized, but that would have insinuated she had done something wrong or didn't want to touch Carmen. But she did want to touch her. And if safety was guaranteed in Carmen's presence, then she wanted to spend more time with her as well.

"Do you run?" Joan suddenly asked. "Usually I work out in the Marmax fitness center, but I like to run on Sundays."

Carmen had seen Joan's hands moving, so she was able to rein in her reaction to the light touch. Her heart skipped a beat or two, but she held it together.

She reminded herself that Joan was a singer, not a threat.

"I can run," she confirmed with a nod. She usually stayed away from it unless it was for a PT test for the military, or if she was preparing herself for the test. But she would go with Joan if that was what the rocker wanted to do.

"You don't mind?" Joan didn't want to force Carmen into something she really didn't want to do. She felt an ever increasing need to show her appreciation for everything Carmen did for her. Sure, the bodyguard was compensated monetarily, but that didn't seem like enough. Joan felt beholden to her, and she didn't know what to do about it.

"Nah, I don't mind," Carmen said with a shake of her head. She glanced over at Joan with a grin and added teasingly, "You'll just have to try and keep up with me." She was used to running miles at a time, she doubted Joan would want to go through that.

"Now, I don't doubt you could kick my ass in the weightlifting department," Joan started to gloat as she looked Carmen up and down, eyes finding lean muscle, "But running's kind of my specialty." She mostly jogged at an even pace while she went out, but she enjoyed sprinting too. It felt like if she went fast enough, far enough – nothing could catch up with her.

There were a few trails she loved to take, scenic routes that traversed through a beautiful San Diego park. She couldn't think of a better way to spend her Sunday morning than running with Carmen in such a place.

Carmen grinned as she got up. "We'll just have to see, won't we?" She picked up the bottle of water and pack of crackers so that Joan could have them in the front seat if she needed them. "Let's get you home."

Joan followed Carmen up to the passenger side of the vehicle and took the food and beverage when it was offered. She was tired, dead tired. But that was a good thing; the best sleep came to her when she was exhausted.

In the SUV, she finished the water before resting her head on an arm and closing her eyes. Joan was safe here with Carmen, she reminded herself – sleep fogging up the corners of her mind. Carmen was a practiced driver, so the ride was a smooth one. Smooth enough that five minutes in, Joan was asleep.

Carmen glanced over when she noticed Joan slump a bit and smiled, unguarded.

When they got back to Joan's building, she came to a stop and turned the vehicle off. She quietly got out of the SUV and walked around to the other side of the vehicle. Slowly and carefully, she opened up the passenger door, putting a hand on Joan's shoulder to make sure she didn't fall over.

"Joan," she whispered, so as not to jar the woman awake. "Let's get you inside."

Joan's eyes slid open, but she wasn't surprised by Carmen this time. In the back of her mind, it was Carmen's presence that lulled her to sleep in the first place. Sleepily, she leapt down from the SUV and felt that terrifying, stomach-dropping sensation of thinking the ground was closer than it actually was. Off by an inch, she gasped and stumbled into Carmen.

"Easy," Carmen said, finding an easy excuse to touch Joan again. She held the woman in her arms until Joan settled and shook her head.

Just because Carmen was her bodyguard, didn't mean Joan had to use her as a literal safety net. "Sorry. I'm more tired than I thought." Bed had just become her top priority.

"Don't worry about it." Carmen went to the back of the SUV and grabbed Joan's guitar, carrying it

100

for her. Joan offered to take her instrument, but after Carmen insisted, the woman gave her an appreciative, drowsy smile. She would have forgotten the guitar in the back of the SUV, she was that tired.

Carmen then led the way inside and to the elevator, taking charge of all of the incredibly difficult tasks – like button-pressing and unlocking doors.

Leaning against one of her entryway walls while Carmen fit her key into the lock, Joan yawned. "What time do you wanna go tomorrow?" She would be certain to set an alarm on her phone before she crashed so she could be up on time to run tomorrow.

Carmen smirked as she perked an eyebrow at Joan. "I don't think rock stars know what five or six a.m. is unless they're up that late. So, let's say eight?" That was much later than she was used to working out, but she would accommodate Joan's schedule. She was working for the rocker after all.

Joan chuckled at the other woman. "Sure, sure. Eight," she confirmed. "I'll be up." She picked herself up from the wall. Blue eyes fluttered from the guitar Carmen set down to the woman herself. "Thank you." Joan didn't nail down her gratitude to any one act, but she was very appreciative.

"You're welcome," Carmen told her with a nod. "Get some rest, and I'll see you in the morning." With that, Carmen turned to leave. She needed some sleep herself, and was ready to collapse in her own bed.

Joan didn't forget to lock the front door this time. She left her guitar case in the entryway and walked back to her bedroom, flipping lights on as she went. She hadn't been living in the penthouse long enough to know her way around in the dark. In a matter of minutes, Joan washed the make-up off of her face, brushed her teeth, and dressed down for bed.

Briefly, she debated turning on the television

in her room for some background noise, but she decided she didn't need it as she rested her head on top of a cool pillow. Her last thoughts of the night were of Carmen. The pitch of her voice, the way she wore her eyeliner with a thin line on the top lid and nothing underneath, how she carried herself. Joan believed the world could sit on Carmen's shoulders, and it still wouldn't make her
slouch.

CHAPTER NINE

It was a quick trip down to the first floor and to the
SUV. Carmen got in and drove back to her own
apartment. She heaved out a sigh as she walked inside,
happy to be home. After bolting the door, she went to
the kitchen and emptied her pockets in their specific
order. Each item was placed with care and precision
before she got herself a glass of water.

Carmen carried the plastic cup of water and
grabbed her handgun, heading into her bedroom. The
gun went into its place in her bedside table, and she
got ready for bed. Down to a pair of boxers and a
tank, she dropped into bed. Having slept on the couch
the night before, her bed felt utterly amazing. She
stretched out, closed her eyes, and tried not to think of
Joan sitting in the spotlight at that bar. For just a
moment, she had wanted to be the only one there.

Seven hours later, her alarm was going off.
This time, she was much more rested and not jarred
awake. Carmen got up and dressed in a pair of
sweatpants and tank top – both of which read,
"USMC" – before pulling her hair into a ponytail. She
got over the compulsion to put it in a military-style
bun. She shut her handgun and pair of handcuff in the
glovebox of the SUV, before going to get her charge
at eight o'clock sharp.

By some miracle, Joan was totally ready to go
before Carmen arrived. Her semi-wild hair was tied
back into a ponytail and her sunglasses were resting on
the neck of her shirt. Carmen had been right; early,
bright morning hours were a plague on her existence,
but Joan found she could tolerate them with the right
amount of protective gear.

Joan made the mistake of not checking to investigate who was at her door before she opened it, but it couldn't have been anyone other than Carmen. Happy to see the other woman, Joan left the penthouse smiling. There was something about Carmen's perfect biceps that made getting up this early worth it.

"Do you know where Adrian Park is?" Joan asked as they got to the black SUV. It was just a few blocks east of the Marmax high-rise, and it had a wonderful selection of dirt trails skirting a myriad of ponds.

"I do." Carmen opened up the door for the singer. "That's where I went to get ready for my last PT test." Dirt trails were definitely different from a track, but it was good practice for timed running. With Joan in the vehicle, Carmen got in as well and headed for the park in question.

Joan furrowed her eyebrows. "I'm sorry," she said quickly. "What's a PT test?" It wasn't an acronym she was familiar with, but she could guess well enough that it had to do with the military.

"It's a test to make sure we still meet the physical requirements of the military," Carmen explained. "Sit ups, pull ups, running three miles... No big deal."

"Oh," Joan drawled while she made a face. She relied more on diet than exercise to stay healthy, so a test of sit ups, pulls ups, and running – no, thanks. "I think I'll stick to singing," She laughed in the kind of carefree way that she thought Stan's terror had chased off.

"I don't know why," Carmen teased with a grin. They came up to the park and she parked the SUV. "Let's go see if you can keep up with me." When they were both out of the vehicle, Carmen locked up and then double-checked to be sure that no one was getting in.

Joan did a few stretches on their way to the track. A few other joggers and a couple of cyclists were spread throughout the small parking lot, all looking to go the same way as Joan and Carmen.

"I hate to break it to you," Joan smirked, "but you wouldn't make a very good bodyguard if you left me in the dust." She was at an advantage here; Carmen could really only go as fast as Joan allowed.

Carmen feigned a pout. "Ah, ruin my fun." She knew she'd have to hold back as soon as she'd agreed to running with Joan. There would be no seven-minute mile here. She was ready to keep pace with her companion, though.

Joan laughed again before breaking out into a run. Normally, she started at a jog, but she was feeling impish and competitive. The trail-goers had a little, unspoken set of guidelines while on the course that Joan had learned through observation. Walkers and slow joggers kept to the right, while the cyclists and runners stayed left – just like they would on the road. But unlike driving, no one suffered any road rage. Most people nodded and said hello to the people they passed. With the coniferous trees, patches of grass, and smell of tepid water, this was a much more pleasant atmosphere.

"Come on!" she called back to Carmen after getting a lead of a few yards.

Carmen grinned and huffed in disbelief. She started off after Joan, not having that hard of a time catching up. The parties and studio were Joan's world, but this was right up the Marine's alley. She wouldn't show off too much, but she might have to indulge in some fun.

The run was an exhilarating way to spend the morning. Every time Joan tried to speed them up,

Carmen matched her steps. Although the woman was a little shorter than Joan, she still managed eat up ground faster than Joan could. Half an hour in, Joan's lungs were in dire straits, but Carmen didn't look winded at all.

Joan let up, reining their speed to something more akin to fast walk. "God- damn- it," she panted when she came to a complete stop. She rested her hands on her knees. "I can't keep going." Joan waved off Carmen, dramatically whining, "Go on without me."

Carmen slowed down and laughed. "Nobody gets left behind," she said, entirely on impulse. "I'll drag you out of here if I have to."

Joan was still trying to catch her breath as she stood up straight and stretched out her back. "Ugh," she complained, disgusted with her lack of fitness. So much for impressing Carmen with that. Her music didn't seem to ensnare the other woman either... What was a girl to do?

"Any chance you want to double as a personal trainer?" Joan was kidding, mostly. She could picture it now: Carmen running down some unidentifiable trail while Joan continuously fell behind – if not because she was tired then because it meant she could stare at Carmen's ass. *Jesus*, Joan thought, *more professionalism – less perv.*

"A personal trainer?" Carmen repeated, quirking a brow. She looked Joan over for a moment – possibly taking her time about it. "I don't know... Think you could handle it?" If Joan wanted to get in shape, that was her prerogative. While Carmen was still working for Joan, she could give pointers.

"If you're going to yell at me like drill sergeants always do in the movies, then no." Behind a relaxed smile, Joan moved to the right side of the dirt trail so people could pass them. She had pretty much

106

reached her limit for the morning, but they were closer to the end if they went forward, not backwards, so she got them moving again.

Joan was about to say something else as they walked, but a melody sounded from one of her pockets. Thinking it was Jerry wanting to talk about how the set at Dodger's went last night, Joan answered without paying attention.

"Hello?"

It had taken quite some time by his standards to get her phone number. But when you knew the right people to put on the job, and enough money was involved – anything was possible. The first time he tried to call, he backed out and hung up quickly.

He was ready now.

And he knew she was ready.

It was time for them to speak. It was time for them to be together. So when she actually answered, his heart stopped and his breath got stuck in his throat. Hearing her voice, speaking directly to him... it wasn't just a song. This was... this was intimate. This was just for them.

"Joan," her name left him in a whisper, but he quickly gathered himself. "Oh, my angel, you don't have to say anything. I know you're with that woman, and you don't want her to know about us. It's all right. Have you read my letters? I'm sure you have. I know you don't want anyone to know about our relationship; I know that's why you don't write back to me. You sing for me instead."

He licked his lips, grabbing the white handle of his knife before continuing. "I forgive you, my angel. Of course I do. I could never stay angry with you for long. I promise we'll be together soon. I know you're looking forward to it as much as I am. I wish I could have seen you at Dodger's last night, I'm sure you were wonderful. Soon, you'll be mine... and I'll be the last person you sing for."

Color drained from the singer's face. She stopped in her tracks and listened to the confession of a madman. What took Stan moments to say took Joan milliseconds to sear into her flesh. He mentioned Carmen, causing Joan to look right at Carmen before she had to compose herself to listen to the rest.

Angel... letters... relationship – the words rotted Joan from the inside out as her hand locked around the iPhone. She couldn't speak back to him; she couldn't tell him to fuck off or get a goddamn life. She couldn't ask for his name or what he wanted. What he wanted was a little too clear.

"Soon, my angel," he repeated. "We won't have to wait much longer."

The line went dead. He pulled the battery out of his disposable cell phone. Both pieces went into the trash before he spun around in his chair to face the poster of Joan on the wall.

"Soon," he whispered to it.

As he stared up at the blue eyes in the picture, he reached into his coat pocket and pulled out two items: a keycard and a key. They were placed on his desk next to the knife.

Carmen stopped when Joan did, frowning when she saw the singer's reaction to the call. Her gut told her what was going on, but she needed to hear it to be sure.

"Joan, what's wrong?"

Joan didn't hear Carmen question her, she couldn't hear anything but the repeating words in her head. It felt like time was stopping. It felt like she was high – on the bad stuff; the stuff that made her paranoid.

"I can't escape..." The phone, and the hand wrapped around it, lowered slowly to Joan's side. She saw with eyes that were not in the present, but the road where her future diverted into infamy. It was in the news articles and the tweets.

Young celebrity life ended by deranged psycho.

Joan Devintia: Murdered at Age 23.

So sad about @joan.devintia #cutshort

The clamor for her unreleased CD would hit a pinnacle by the time her funeral rolled around. The record label would go over Jerry's head and release it in its current state. It would go platinum in the first week for the simple, macabre fact that there would never be any more music from the singer. People who hadn't met her before would cry. Close friends would tweet meaningful messages – in 140 characters or less. And a percentage of the demented public would label the killer a hero. Celebrities weren't real people; they were shadows and lies, idols composed of drug-abuse, and greed without a soul.

Or, she could go the other way. She could be forgotten, ignored... Her music could disappear forever. Which was the better fate, she couldn't say.

Joan suddenly pushed the phone into Carmen's hands. She didn't want anything more to do with this, or Stan the Stalker, and things like going out and taking calls only served her on a silver platter.

Carmen took the phone, knowing all too well what happened even though Joan hadn't rightly answered her. It had been the stalker who called and talked directly to Joan. What he said obviously had an effect – she swore she could see Joan shaking. Without questioning the action, she slid the phone into her pocket – it was going to turn into another item she gave Sam for the case. Jerry could get his client a new one.

Slowly and carefully, so as not to freak Joan out more than she already was, Carmen reached up to make Joan look at her. "Focus," she requested. "You're here with me. I'm not going to let him anywhere near you. I promised to keep you safe, remember? I keep my promises."

As if someone struck a match against the side of Joan's cheek, fire raced from the spot straight to her heart. Again, it was while Carmen touched her. She searched Carmen's face for comfort and she found it in a serious stare.

"He's coming. He knows *everything*. He knew about my performance last night," Joan rambled. "He knows about you." Carmen could only keep her attention for so long. Joan began to look around, searching the park for anyone watching her. A lone, male runner was approaching from the east. The sun was just behind him, shielding his face from view. It could be him; it could be Stan. Struck with fright, Joan stepped back to let him pass.

Carmen watched blue eyes wildly dart around them, looking for the source of the unnamed threat to her life. "Joan." Carmen said the other woman's name with authority to bring her back to attention. "I want you to listen to me very carefully. You are safe with me. Nothing is going to happen while I'm around." She knew she needed to get Joan somewhere that she felt safe before another anxiety attack struck – if Joan wasn't already in the beginnings of one. "We're going to go back to the SUV, and I'll take you back home, all right? I'll even stay for a while if you want me to."

If safety was anything like privacy in a celebrity's life, then there was no place safe for Joan – with Carmen or without. The familiar setting of home was comforting though. That was the place Joan

110

wanted to be. She couldn't freak out here in public, though she very much wanted to.

Part of her wished she would have taken some form of self-defense class like she planned to... before. But Joan knew that kind of physicality just wasn't her. The only time she interacted with violence was when it was inflicted on her.

Joan stayed close to the bodyguard, closer than was polite but this was a special circumstance. As the two walked back to the SUV, Joan ground her teeth and bit her lip in a constant state of stress.

Carmen kept a hand on Joan's back, leading Joan to the SUV. She got the startled woman inside, then got into the vehicle herself. Without a word of explanation, she pulled out an extra key after starting the car – this key hadn't been on a ring with the others. She leaned across Joan, unlocking the glove compartment and opening it to retrieve the gun and handcuffs from its secure spot.

Before settling back into her seat, Carmen adjusted herself so she could wrap the belt of the holster around her waist and put it into place on her back – tucked away out of sight beneath her sweat pants. The handcuffs went into one of her pockets before starting the car.

Joan's heart fluttered violently at the sight of a gun. Eying the other woman so much in the past, Joan had caught sight of the holster before, but she never saw the pistol. She wasn't sure if the presence of a firearm made her feel better or worse.

Once they pulled into the parking garage, Carmen scanned the area before they got out. She ushered Joan inside, taking her up to the penthouse. She didn't want Joan to turn into a recluse, but she was certain that her charge would want the safe familiarity of her home. She planned on sticking around for a little while this time around, until she was sure Joan had settled back down.

Joan was shaking by the time she stepped foot into her apartment. "Will you check- Please?" The elevator ride made her very much aware that if Stan knew her phone number, then he probably knew where she lived. It would still be impossible for him to get this far into her penthouse, but Carmen had the unfortunate position of guard dog and gerbil.

She pointed toward the rest of the apartment to get her meaning across as she stayed close to the door. She wasn't going any further until she knew the place was empty.

Carmen nodded as she stepped further into the apartment. "You stay right there," she told the blonde. She went through the penthouse, checking every room, nook, and cranny that could be housing a psychopathic stalker. When she was satisfied the apartment hadn't been tampered with, she returned to Joan.

"It's all clear," she said. "Just the two of us here."

Joan's eyes fluttered as relief swept over her. The sensation was short-lived, but it was enough to get some answers.

"What letters?" she asked Carmen. While Joan had a few fans that wrote more than once, she doubted that she had read anything like what she heard over the phone. Carmen was in charge of her security, so if any threatening notes had come down the line – Carmen and Jerry would know about it. "He talked about letters."

Of course he talked about the letters. With a sigh, Carmen bid Joan to come further into the penthouse.

"Let's sit down," she said, drawing her into the living room. "The guy sent letters to you – Jerry

112

held them back so you wouldn't have to see them. A couple of days ago, he passed them on to me."

"What do they say?" Joan asked, hoping Carmen would divulge the information without a fight.

Carmen was in a catch-22; if she told Joan the truth, the woman would freak out. And if she avoided the question, Joan would know that it was bad. She took a moment to weigh her options and figure out which was the lesser of two evils.

"I agree with Jerry on this one... I think it's better that you don't know," she finally answered.

Joan flashed glacial eyes at Carmen. She didn't see how that was their call to make. Jerry and Carmen were both in it for the money, Joan was in it because this was her life. There was one easy way around this. If Carmen wouldn't tell her, then she would call Jerry.

"Give me back my phone, please." Hand thrust out for the device, Joan felt her patience dwindle.

Carmen felt bad about keeping the truth from Joan. She believed it was necessary, though. This was some deep shit surrounding the rock star. She hesitated for a moment, then pulled the phone out of her pocket and offered it to Joan.

The second that plastic hit skin, Joan stood up with the phone and called Jerry. She walked into the other room as she waited for her manager to pick up. It was a rare day when the man didn't answer his phone, but it was also Sunday and he usually reserved that for his family.

Carmen sat and waited while Joan was on the phone with her manager. She shot a text off to Sam, letting him know that a call had been made by the stalker. The only good thing about this was that the police could start getting more involved.

Joan wasn't on the line long, for all the good it did. Even after explaining the situation to Jerry, he

113

wouldn't reveal the contents of the letters either. It was frustrating to say the least. Joan forgot the three P's of a good career as she ended the call.

"Keeping me in the dark isn't going to keep him from coming after me, Jerry! Christ!" That rocker attitude was showing off in a bad way, but people tended to cling to boisterous actions when their life was threatened. "No... No! How am I supposed to calm down when this fucker is calling me on an unlisted number? ... Yeah," she said sarcastically. "I might be there tomorrow – if I'm not dead."

Joan slammed her phone onto the kitchen counter along with both of her hands. She was hot... and tired... and scared. Carmen appeared in the doorway a moment later, but Joan didn't look at her.

"Joan," Carmen said, trying to announce herself even though they both knew she was there. "I know you're upset, but Jerry and I did what we did for your good. The police have a case building against your stalker, and that's where the letters went. A friend of mine is a sergeant in the department. He's personally handling the case."

"Save it," the woman snapped, keeping her eyes closed tight. After a month of terror, she couldn't take much more. "Get out," she threatened, her once beautiful voice twisted by an unspoken past. She couldn't do this again; she couldn't do another obsessed, violent man with an extra dose of mental instability.

"Joan," Carmen repeated the woman's name apologetically. Leave it to the stalker to break everything apart. "If you really want me to leave... I will. But what Jerry and I did was to protect you, not to hurt you."

Joan shook her head, disagreeing with Carmen on such a fundamental level it deconstructed everything she thought about the bodyguard. She

114

didn't feel protected, she felt lied to. Which was borderline bullshit since she couldn't lie to save her own damn skin. Stan was scary enough without having to know that others knew more about him than she did, and Carmen was one of them.

"I'll see you tomorrow," Joan said with a certain amount of finality.

Carmen hesitated for a few moments, trying to think of a reason to stay and try to smooth things over. Nothing came to mind, and she finally turned to leave. She couldn't stay if she wasn't welcome to, and Joan had her phone number if something came up.

She walked out the front door, locking it behind herself. Although she could understand why Joan was upset, she wished the rocker would trust her enough to handle the situation. Reading those letters would have only scared Joan more. The ride down to the first floor seemed to take an eternity, and she was thankful when the doors opened, letting her return to her SUV so she could go home.

Joan spent the next hour pacing, throwing up, showering, and crying – in that order, to be repeated as she felt necessary. Her nerves were frayed and on their way to shot, but she knew a way to fix this. Okay, maybe not fix but at least make the situation tolerable. It was sitting in one of her drawers in small, unmarked, plastic bags.

Late in the afternoon, Joan couldn't hold out any longer. She cut a line of cocaine on a handheld mirror from inside her purse. She snorted the powder, thinking about the relief it would bring. Joan grew up knowing drugs were never the answer to problems. She went through the standard D.A.R.E. program in school. She was sat down by her parents – now happily retired in Florida – to talk about what having a future meant. Her first boyfriend had been strictly against them and booze of any kind until they were both legal.

And then she met David. His stash of opiates was the only remedy for the pain he inflicted on her.

Her music came from personal experience; it came from bruises and name-calling; from late nights and passionate ones. It trickled down from ultra-stellar highs and welled up from self-defining lows. It was everything she was in the moment, and it brought upon her the worst hell she could imagine. Stan was her punishment, her salvation, and – ironically – he could end the pain better than any opiate.

CHAPTER TEN

Carmen went home and showered, but she couldn't sit still. She wasn't in control of her situation or her work. Just a few years ago, not being in control ended in people dying. Carmen screwed up her job – and it was for the worst. Shellshock was threatening to creep up on her for the first time in months.

With a slightly shaking hand, she reached into her pocket and pulled out her phone, dialing a familiar number. A couple rings in, the man answered and Carmen finally took a full breath.

"Macrae."

"Sam. Can I come over?"

"Of course. What's wrong?" he asked, voice all concern.

"Today's rough... I need some help."

"Come on over."

The two hung up and Carmen had to check her pockets three times before she could walk out the door. It was a quick drive to the man's house, and she practically jumped out of the SUV. Sam was sitting on the front porch, dogs out playing in the yard.

He got up when Carmen got out of her vehicle, walking over to open up the gate for her. "Hey."

"Look at you, dressed up like a civilian," Carmen teased with a grin, looking him over as she stepped into the yard. He was actually wearing shorts – probably the first time since they'd been on inactive duty. "Not many guys can make a prosthetic look badass." Where she now saw carbon fiber and polyurethane, she had seen blood and torn flesh once. Sam had lost his leg from the knee down.

"Yeah? I think so, too," he said, watching as the two pit bulls ran over to maul the woman with unconditional affection.

Carmen knelt down, one hand on each of the large beasts. She was nearly knocked over by the brutes as noses and slobbery tongues were pushed into her face.

"I'm happy to see you guys, too," she assured them.

"All right, all right," Sam addressed the animals. "Let her get up before you drown her in slobber."

Carmen stood after that, walking with Sam to sit on the front porch. Excited by a familiar person, the dogs ran off to chase each other through the yard. Her gaze followed them for a moment before she looked down at the phone she pulled from her pocket. No notifications from Joan, and her volume was still up. Nothing had changed since the last time she checked.

"Going to tell me what's up?" Sam asked after long moments of silence.

"Joan found out about the letters. She's pissed because we won't tell her what's in them." Carmen fidgeted until her phone was resting just right in her pocket again. "And when the stalker called her, she freaked out. This situation is going downhill – fast."

"You can only do so much," Sam pointed out.

"It's like when we were on deployment, Sam. I mess this up much more, somebody's going to die."

"Everybody makes mistakes, Savedra. Nothing you ever did while we were out there got anybody killed... but you did save my life."

"Couldn't save your leg, though."

"What's a leg compared to years of life?" he questioned as he leaned in. "Second guessing yourself – that's always been your problem."

Carmen shrugged, and then began to pet the blue pit bull that had finally settled next to her. The animal had an extraordinary calming effect. She never could understand why the breed got such a bad rap. They were the sweetest dogs she had ever met.

Sam nudged Carmen with his arm. "You're good at what you do. You'll keep her safe. It sounds like you were right – she's fragile. This is some heavy shit. Add the pressure of rising fame, and it's a lot to handle for the passionate heart of a musician."

Carmen's lips turned into a light smile. "Passionate heart of a musician?" She shook her head at the memory of Sam pulling out his guitar while on base. "What part of playing the same fucking song over and over again makes you a passionate musician?" The music was comforting, the first few times.

Sam barked a laugh, catching the happy attention of his dogs. "It was the only song I knew from start to finish!"

Carmen chuckled before her eyes softened and focused on the animal at her side. "You're right, Sam," she replied after a moment's pause. "All I can do is my job."

"That's all any of us can do. Now... Maria's putting lunch together. Why don't you stay and eat with us? She was upset that she didn't get to see you the other night."

Carmen nodded and got up with Sam. She tried to relax while spending some time with him and his family.

~*~

Joan did just enough coke to remove herself from the edge of nightmares and paranoia. She felt like she could write a thousand songs about the situation.

As she sat on the hard-wood floor in the living room, guitar by her leg, papers scattered about – she wrote lyrics. She wrote for hours; scratching out previous lines, revising and editing, over and over.

All in all, it was hard to say if any of the pseudo-songs could be salvaged into good music. The themes and language were dark, even for her, but it helped pass the time.

It was approaching four in the morning when Joan decided to take a sedative and laid down on her couch. She didn't set an alarm. Hell, her phone could have been dead for all she knew. She really didn't care if she woke up when she was supposed to or not; she just wanted to rest. The singer fell asleep with a mess on the floor and the TV droning on about fitness equipment.

~*~

Carmen wasn't expecting the scene she found waiting for her the next morning. "Joan?"

Her name spoken, Joan was pulled from the far, dark recess of her mind. Draped in a sedate fog, she didn't open her eyes. Nothing could be important enough to fully wake up. She was locked in a dream, paralyzed from her eyelids down. Whatever entity was calling to her would have to come back later.

Carmen sighed and pocketed her keys, careful not to step on any papers as she crossed the living room. She knelt down next to the couch, knowing that it would be unsettling for Joan to wake to someone leaning over her.

"Joan, come on, time to get up." At this rate, they were going to be late.

That nagging voice came back stronger this time, as if someone was right next to Joan. She struggled to wake but managed to open her sleepy

120

eyes. The first thing she saw made her want to close them again. It was Carmen. The bodyguard was here, in her penthouse, because it was time to go the studio. And Joan had spent last night binging and angry.

With heavy limbs, she sat up on the couch and took deep, calming breaths through her nose. Air hit her nostrils like ice, freezing and cracking dry skin. Gravity pulled a rivulet of blood from her nose. Joan lifted a hand to her face and covered the tips of her fingers in warm, liquid shame so she could see it.

Carmen turned and grabbed a tissue from the box on the coffee table, then righted herself to face Joan again. She tried to leave her eyes empty of judgement as she reached up, and first wiped the blood off of Joan's finger, then dabbed away the red trail that had been left behind under her nose.

Joan placed a hand over Carmen's so she could keep the tissue in place herself. There were no harsh words from Carmen despite her threat that there would be hell to pay for future drug use. Joan didn't know what to make of that. Was Carmen all talk? Did she really not care what the singer did to herself? Or did she realize how hard yesterday had been and didn't want to compact a lecture on top of it?

Joan didn't know, and she wasn't going to ask after Carmen placed a hand on her leg.

"You know... when I came back from deployment, I was a wreck." Carmen paused as she gathered the courage to face the memories. "You wouldn't believe how many nights I spent with a gun pressed to my temple. I couldn't leave my home. I was so paranoid that I was sure there was someone with a grenade, or gun, or pipe bomb around every single corner. I couldn't drive anywhere, because I *knew* there were IEDs along the road. I'd go for days, unable to sleep because of night terrors."

She stopped again to think over her next

words. What would Sam say? What had Sam said to her in the past? Emotions were universal, even if experiences were not.

"You can't let your demons win. They don't define who you are."

Joan was struck by an unnatural warmth as Carmen spoke. She thought she knew the face of fear, but like Stan's shadowed features, her impression lacked the finer details that she could fight this. Someone had survived it, and that woman was kneeling right in front of her with a gentle hand on her leg and compassion in dark brown eyes.

Joan was quiet, but not without reaction. She lowered the tissue from her face, feeling that her nose had stopped bleeding. A tear dropped from the corner of her eye, and then another. She wouldn't torture herself with comparisons; everyone had personal demons, and if Joan's monsters didn't define her, then neither did Carmen's.

"I'm scared," Joan finally whispered.

For the first time in ages, Carmen felt her heart ache for someone. Joan was only a few years younger than herself, and yet the gap felt wider than that. Different lives did that, but somehow, two completely different paths still led to the exact same spot.

She reached up to wipe away the tears that had spilled down Joan's cheeks. "I know you are," she told Joan. "But I've got your back. I'm not going to let him hurt you."

Joan turned her face in toward Carmen's hand, soaking up the feel of comfort. She closed her eyes and spoke without thinking.

"Where were you a couple of years ago?"
Jesus. I can't put that on Carmen. Joan made a sour face at herself as she got up. She wiped her eyes and turned away. If Carmen asked, she would explain, but she was

122

running late and emotions were already soaring high enough. "I should get ready."

Carmen stood as Joan did. "Go ahead," she said with a nod. "I'll call Jerry and let him know we're going to be a little late."

Joan retreated to her bedroom. She spent the most time washing her face, praying it would wake her up and make her look like she had spent another tame night in her penthouse instead of the drug-addled evening she put herself through. Between changing her clothes and reapplying her make-up, she wondered if she could have called Carmen to come over when she was debating between getting high and staying sober.

While Joan was getting herself ready, Carmen pulled out her phone and called Jerry. The manager attempted to get all puffed up about them being late and how unprofessional it was, but the bodyguard shot him down and got on his case for not being understanding of the situation. He quickly retreated from Carmen's fiery defense of the rocker. However, he did tell her that another letter had arrived that morning.

CHAPTER ELEVEN

In her usual jeans and tight-fitting shirt, Joan came back ready to go. Ashamed of herself and apologetic, but ready.

Carmen immediately took notice of her. She walked over to Joan and reached out to fix a shirt sleeve that had gotten ruffled while the woman dressed.

"There you go," she said with an approving nod. "Ready?"

"As I'll ever be," Joan responded softly. She locked them out of the penthouse, leaving her mess for later. She didn't want to compound her lateness by eating up more time, which of course, meant she didn't eat food either. Maybe she could convince the guys to go to lunch early.

Carmen led the way down to the SUV. Once they were in the vehicle, she drove them to the studio. Jerry had told her they'd be working on a music video that day, so it would probably be a long one. She would make sure that Joan ate within the next couple of hours, knowing without a doubt that she hadn't eaten anything in a while. At some point, while Joan was busy during the day she'd slip away to get the letter that had arrived, too.

Jerry didn't look very happy when Joan finally managed to show up. It was day one of the music video shoot for *Snowball Earth's* first single, "Volcano." Though the crew was fairly small, everyone was waiting on Joan. She was rushed to hair and make-up, while Jerry went over the finalized script with her. It had been decided that the choreographed fight would be trimmed down to a few moves and shot with a slow-motion camera on Tuesday.

While Joan was talking to the director, Carmen pulled Jerry aside and they went to his office to retrieve the letter he'd informed her about. Now that she knew about these notes, she decided to carry a pair of gloves on her during the week – just in case. She slid the gloves out of her pocket and pulled them on before handling the letter. Carmen opened the envelope and withdrew a cutout section of a restaurant menu.

Dearest,

You shouldn't let Rory talk you into such nasty habits. Your body is a temple – it's my temple. If you continue to desecrate that temple, I'll have no choice but to destroy it.

Take better care of yourself, my angel, so when the time comes I can worship you properly.

"¡*Ay, mierda*!" she swore loudly, having to stop herself from throwing the appetizer menu on the ground out of frustration. This guy had been at Prestige the night they were there, and she had no clue. "*¡Cabrón!*"

She slid the note back into the envelope and put it into her back pocket before she headed out of Jerry's office. She went back down to the studio where the video was going to be shot, so she could keep an eye on things and hoped that Joan would feel better with her there.

The band was going to shoot the video for the song in reverse, starting with the end since it would require the most production. The make-up artist had touched up Joan's application and added color. On top of that, grey powder was smeared on her face. It looked like she had just escaped a house fire by the time the artist was done. In singed, black plaid, Joan walked on set. The band was in costume, mulling about the stage in front of a green screen.

Joan took her position and grabbed the microphone from the stand. She only had to lip sync as the song played in the background, but Jerry advised her to sing along with it. It would look more believable that way, so she took deep breaths, reserving her air for a strong open. The director gave a few instructions, then the music started playing – thirty seconds before the part they wanted to capture. When the camera rolled, Joan stared it down.

> "*I hear you coming*
> *I watch you blow!*
> *Won't see me running*
> *Won't scream no!*"

Singing without having to worry about how she sounded was therapeutic for her. A fake snow machine was throwing grey flurries into the air. Blanketed in pseudo ash, Joan put everything she had into making this shoot look real. She dug up old memories and let them roll over her. Snarling and screaming at the mic, she was an animal. She was everything the music called for.

Hanging around with the crew while they were shooting the video, Carmen kept a special eye on the microphone, expecting it to melt in Joan's hands. There was definitely enough intensity for it.

When the director stopped production for a break, Joan slumped into a nearby chair. Crew members were filing out to take their lunch hour, while Joan wouldn't be allowed to leave. She could spare about twenty minutes to eat before she had to go back into hair and make-up for touch ups.

Carmen walked over to her charge and offered a white paper bag. "Here, *chica*, you need to eat." She had called in an order for Joan and had it delivered ten minutes ago. There was a sandwich on ciabatta bread inside the bag, with some freshly made kettle cooked chips to accompany it. The meal was decidedly difficult to order. Something about staring at the restaurant menu after it downloaded onto her phone was off-putting.

"Oh, thanks," Joan said in surprise. Maybe it was the music being played so loudly, or just the consistency of unhealthy thoughts between her ears that made her momentarily deaf, but she hadn't heard the other woman coming. Smiling, she opened the take-out. She was about to run over to the vending machines, but real food was much better.

"You're welcome," Carmen said with a nod. She took a seat next to the rocker just as she caught Jerry's assistant coming toward them out of the corner of her eye. The paperboard takeout container in his hand was a minute too late.

"Joan, I've got lunch- Oh, I see you're taken care of." Kevin held the warm food closer to himself.

Maybe he was using the steam to keep his dress shirt from creasing.

Carmen smirked at him, content with how disappointed he looked.

Between bites, Joan nodded. "Yeah, sorry, Kenny."

"Again, it's Kevin."

Joan grimaced as Kevin's face reddened. The young man had been Jerry's assistant for the last three months, but when they met – she thought he said his name was Kenny and it stuck.

"Shit," she scolded herself. "I know that. I'm sorry."

First impressions were hard to veer away from. Carmen's idea of Kevin was stained with the kind of dislike that made her happy Joan couldn't get his name right. Kevin's ego must have suffered a massive blow if his expression was any indication. Getting the brush off from a hot rock star must have hurt, and Carmen wondered… if it hurt enough to make him do something about it. One small slight from a celebrity was more than enough to make an enemy for life.

Kevin shrugged and half-smiled. "It's not my name that matters in this relationship." His tone was non-threatening. If anything, he sounded a lot like Jerry. "If you need anything else, let me know." Joan nodded before Kevin walked away.

When Joan had eaten most of her food, she glanced over at Carmen. "Director says we're doing one more scene today. Just me," she explained. "And I don't feel like going back to the studio, so you can call it a day after that." After Carmen took her back to her penthouse, of course.

Carmen cleared her throat before speaking. "Okay, sounds good." This was turning out to be a pretty easy day – just standing around in an air conditioned building, listening to music. Later, she would just have to take the newest letter to Sam, so he could add it to the evidence pile.

Joan thanked Carmen again for the meal before she was due back. After touch ups, Joan stood in front of the green screen alone. The guys had gone home since Joan decided this was it for the day. There was a limited number of takes the director could get of the next shot before Joan would have to quit. No one wanted her to hurt herself, so Jerry capped them at three. Three tries, and if the director couldn't get what he wanted out of that, they would have to come up with something else.

Joan was handed a prop by an assistant. Between her fingers was a silver, ornate torch, and on a rocky-looking pedestal beside her was a glass of paraffin. The assistant lit the torch and quickly backed away as the director yelled.

"Fire on set!" The man hollered the same thing over his shoulder before turning back to the singer. "All right. Ready, Joan?" Between watching people pick up fire extinguishers and knowing exactly what would happen if things went south, she nodded. "Action." There were no musical cues Joan had to meet; all of that would be done in editing. The only thing she was responsible for was breathing fire.

Joan took a large breath before pouring the lamp oil into her mouth. She tilted her head up at an angle and spit the liquid with force. A fireball burst from the torch and cascaded upwards and outwards as Joan exhausted her breath and her fuel. She held off taking in any more air for a couple of seconds until she was sure it was safe.

"Cut!" When the director halted production, people clapped. It was an impressive, dangerous feat, and it was something Joan taught herself so she could stand out in the industry.

With the warnings and visual cues, Carmen knew something obviously dangerous was coming. Something involving fire was coming. Surely it couldn't be that bad. This was just a music video, after all. Most of the visuals would be added through CGI.

Suddenly, though, there was a ball of fire that put her in the backseat of a Humvee in the middle of flipping over. The flashback lasted for the barest of seconds, but it was more than enough to set her on edge. Her hands clenched tightly into fists and she grated her teeth. She shifted her weight uncomfortably, desperately trying to rein herself in.

Keep it together, Savedra. It's a little bit of fire. You're in the middle of San Diego, for Christ's sake.

After a moment, she turned to leave the space. Fire, she was fine with: fireplaces, grills, candles, lighters. Fireballs, though… those were a different beast – one she hadn't needed to face. While she didn't let herself sink completely into a panic attack, she knew that she did need to get some fresh air before it came to that.

The assistant returned to take the torch from Joan and gave her a bottle of water to wash her mouth out with as well as an empty cup. Joan stepped off set so she could rinse. The director was bugging her for one more take, but she caught sight of Carmen walking toward the exit on the far side of the studio.

"Yeah, sure. Whatever," Joan waved the man off, blue eyes intent of the retreating figure. "Just give me five minutes." As she moved to follow Carmen, she opened the bottle and poured some water into her mouth, steps growing larger with every stride.

She found Carmen standing outside the building. Joan probably looked like quite the sight – fake ash on her face and in her hair, while she wore burnt clothes. It donned on her that something sent

Carmen away, and when she realized what it was – she felt awful for triggering the Marine like that.

Leaning against the building, arms crossed and eyes closed, Carmen took slow, deep inhales of air. The sounds of the city helped keep her rooted in the present – drowning out the screams of agony and explosions that threatened to drag her under. She focused on the car horns, traffic, and people walking past.

"Hey," Joan called quietly, keeping her distance. She didn't want to startle the other woman.

Carmen opened her eyes and glanced over at Joan. "Hey. Shouldn't you be inside doing another take?"

"In five." Joan got closer to Carmen but left a couple of yards between them. "I wanted to make sure you were okay." She could only imagine what was going through Carmen's mind. The gauntlet of past memories could be a terrible place to be when you had war to fall back on.

Carmen nodded, hoping the action seemed more reassuring than she felt. "Oh, yeah, I'm fine," she said, brushing off the incident as if it was nothing. "Just needed a little fresh air after being inside all day."

"Oh..." Joan wrapped her arms around herself and leaned against the wall like Carmen was. She wasn't sure she really believed Carmen, but she wasn't going to press for a reaction. If Carmen wasn't freaking out, then that was good thing. After a minute of steady silence, Joan looked over her shoulder.

"Will you do me a favor? I left some notes in the live room on Friday," she explained. "I'd be really grateful if you got them for me. My legs are killing me from our run." She laughed at herself. "And I just don't think I can do stairs today." Joan prayed her lie was convincing for once. She didn't leave anything in the floor above, but if Carmen was busy retrieving imaginary notes then she wouldn't have to watch Joan spit fire again. Despite what the bodyguard said, Joan still wanted to protect her.

"*And* you want me to be your personal trainer," Carmen teased. "Yeah, I'll get them." She had no reason not to believe what Joan had told her. She was glad for an excuse to stay out of the studio where the video was being shot. It wouldn't take her too long and she would still be in the building if something happened to come up.

"You know how celebrities are," Joan joked back. "They think 'No' means 'Yes' and 'Fuck no' means 'The Starbucks is going to be late.' I'll see you inside." Joan picked herself up off the wall with a grin, knowing full well that she wouldn't see the other woman back in the studio for at least the next ten minutes.

The director wasn't amused by the impromptu break, but Joan was enthused to get this done when she got back. After a few instructions, Joan set up to spit fire again. This time she would be blowing the flame toward the cameras. She wasn't nervous about repeating the move. Things had gone wrong in the past. She had the burn scar on her right hand to prove it, but she learned from the mistake.

After Joan disappeared, Carmen headed back into the building. She went up to the recording studio to look for the notes that Joan had requested.

Inside the live room, she saw a whole lot of nothing. She thought on it a moment before smiling. Joan had called her bluff and gave her a reason not to return to the taping area. Carmen shook her head as she walked back out of the recording studio, taking her time as she went back downstairs. Even if the recording was done by the time she got back down there, Joan would still have to clean up and change her clothes.

When Joan completed the shot, she was excused from the stage and released into wardrobe's capable hands. Behind a screen, the woman took off the costume and put on her old clothes. Her face was still a mess so she took some wipes from the little make-up area and cleaned herself just well enough to look presentable.

Right on cue, Carmen came back to the studio. Joan was a little too happy to see her, grinning as Carmen approached her. Shouldn't she have been disappointed that Carmen couldn't find those mysterious, wandering notes?

Probably.

"Found those notes," Carmen lied, reaching behind herself as if to get them. She pulled her hand back out – obviously with nothing in it. "You should have told me they'd be nearly *impossible* to find." She was grateful for what Joan had done, even though she'd been sent on a wild goose chase.

Joan choked out a fast laugh. "Busted."

"Yeah, you are," Carmen confirmed with a smile. She would have to remember to thank Joan later. "Ready to get out of here?"

Joan didn't answer and instead led Carmen out. They ran into Jerry on the way so she talked shop for a minute. Her manager reminded her how important tomorrow was and all but begged her to be punctual. She would have to do better this time, she knew.

Inside the SUV, waiting for the AC to cool down, Carmen looked over at Joan. "So, I've decided that you could use some company up in that big penthouse of yours this evening. Have you ever had homemade empanadas?" She didn't want Joan to fall back on drugs again.

"I can't say I have," Joan answered. She wasn't sure what to make of Carmen inviting herself

134

over, but Joan figured that having her company would be better than being alone. In truth, she hadn't charged her phone today in fear of what might be on the device. But if Carmen was in the penthouse with her, maybe she could find the courage to plug the iPhone in.

"Good. Then you can't say others you've had are better than mine," Carmen said with a grin. She pulled the SUV away from the parking garage, so they could make a quick pit stop at a grocery store before heading back to Joan's penthouse. Carmen knew she was presuming a lot, inviting herself over – but again, she was charged not only with the singer's safety, but also her wellbeing. This evening, she was just going above and beyond to ensure it.

CHAPTER TWELVE

Joan didn't ask Carmen to check the penthouse this time around. Instead, she walked a bag of groceries into the kitchen, and then returned to the living room to clean up. There were scribbled lyric notes everywhere. Some were nonsensical, some were probably brilliant, but she wasn't going to take the time to go through them right now. She had company; beautiful, black-haired, tan-skinned company.

Carmen stayed in the kitchen, unpacking ingredients she bought while Joan stayed locked in the blacked-out SUV. She set to work, since it would take some time to make the food. She had filling to cook up, pastry to lay out, and utensils to find. Usually she would make the puff pastry from scratch, but that would take far too long.

Finding her way around the kitchen, she gathered the pans that she needed. Her first main objective was to get the meat and vegetables cooking together. Operation Enduring Comfort would never succeed without proper filling.

Joan eventually found her way back to Carmen. She sat at the island in the middle of the room and connected her phone to the charger she always left there. With a little bit of juice running through the system, she turned the device on and watched it quietly. It went through the normal start-up, connected to the network, and auto-updated the operating system.

Her hands started to grow cold as she waited for a notification from an unknown number. Joan looked from the bright screen to Carmen, back to the phone again.

Carmen noticed the attention and glanced over at the boxes of puff pastry that were unopened on the counter. "Hey, Joan? Mind giving me a hand?"

Anxiously, Joan's eyes drifted from the speaker back to her phone. She still hadn't received any notifications, but the device was only halfway through the update. Hadn't the damn thing just updated last week? After a moment's debate, she got to her feet and maneuvered around the island to help.

"What can I do?"

"Would you start unpacking the pastry?" Carmen requested. "It needs to sit out for a little while, before I do anything with it." It was something she could have easily done on her own, but she planned to dole out tasks until Joan was sufficiently distracted.

While empanadas weren't all that difficult, it did take some time to make them. When the filling was done, Carmen started spooning it into the pastry shells – having Joan fold the pastry and pinch it together on the edges. With each shell filled, Carmen took the task of frying them all up. The hot oil made quick work of the pastries.

While Joan was free for a moment, she went back to her device and woke it up. Aside from a few missed calls from numbers she knew well, there was nothing. She carried that relief with her while the two woman sat together and ate.

When they were done, Joan passed Carmen and took away the empty plates. "Does this mean you're my personal chef now, too?" she teased. "Because that was delicious."

"I don't think so." Carmen grinned. "But I'm glad you liked it." She watched Joan take their dirty dishes back into the kitchen, and patiently waited for her to return. There was something that Joan had said to her earlier, which she wanted to know about. The two went and settled on the couch to recover from the excess of food. That was when Carmen made her move.

"Earlier, you said you wished I'd been around a couple years ago... Why?"

Right. Joan had said that this morning, and it was still true. She scratched the back of her neck as she settled on what to tell the other woman. She owed Carmen an explanation, and she trusted her not to go to the press. Legally binding confidentially agreement aside.

Sitting forward on the couch, Joan looked down at the polish on her fingernails. It was time for a fresh application. It was time to tell someone the truth about David.

"About a year after high school... I began dating this guy, David. I had a job as a waitress in my hometown, and he had a place of his own, so I moved in with him. Things were fine for a while. He always disappeared around noon and returned in the evening, sometimes really late, but he wouldn't tell me what he was up to. Just that he was earning money, and I didn't have to work anymore. Despite the fact that I knew better, I quit my job. I relied solely on him for everything, and that was just how he wanted it." Joan took a deep breath, knowing what was coming. She was too far in to stop telling Carmen now.

"He got violent. I wanted out, but I was too proud to go to my parents. They didn't like David, and I kinda burned that bridge when I moved in with him. When he vanished, I walked to town to try and find another job. If I could just get some income, I knew I would be okay. The restaurant took me back, and I was *so* happy to work again. I had plans to put up with David's shit until I had enough cash to get my own place.

"A few days later, David noticed I was

sneaking out to work. He was furious. He beat me, thinking there was no way I'd go to work with a black eye. The joke was on him, though. The next day, I received three times the amount of the tips." Joan smiled lightly as she remembered the kindness of others. She pointed to the right side of her head, running her fingers over the short hair of her undercut. "He held me down and cut my hair. That was my lowest point, when I realized I didn't care if I had enough money – I was gone. I packed everything I owned when he left that afternoon. I shaved my head like this to spite him, and when he got home, the cops were waiting for him.

"He's in prison now," she admitted. "Possession with intent to sell."

The long-winded speech left Joan exhausted. Her story extended beyond that point; she left Florida for California, hunting for a new life. She mended things with her parents, and she molded herself a career from the bones of her memories. But to have Carmen around then... Joan could have used someone watching her back.

Carmen reached over and placed a hand on Joan's knee – physical reassurances were getting easier every day she spent with Joan. She wouldn't have guessed that Operation Enduring Comfort would extend to a past like this, though. Domestic violence was an all too common occurrence in the country, and too few victims of violence had the ability to get out of the situation. Thinking back to a couple of years ago, she wouldn't have been much help to Joan. But she was here now, and that was the important part.

"I'm glad you got out," she said. "That took a lot of courage."

Now that she knew some of Joan's past, it was easy to see why this stalker situation would affect her as badly as it did. Joan already had one man in her life that was abusive, and now there was another threatening her with violence, too. What if they were the same man, and Joan just didn't realize it?

"I promised myself I'd never rely on anyone like that ever again," Joan replied. No matter where her rock star career went, she was going to be a working woman. She didn't mean to ignore Carmen's words, she just didn't know what to say to them. It didn't feel like courage at the time.

"Well, from where I'm sitting, it looks like you're doing pretty good with that," Carmen pointed out, before looking around the penthouse.

Joan followed Carmen's lead, looking around at her place. Carmen was right, she had come far.

After relaxing into the couch, Joan noticed that there was still a hand on her knee. The sight and feel of Carmen's touch brought her immature attraction to Carmen to the forefront of her senses. Joan swallowed down her nerves, realizing this was meant to be a comforting action. *Get it together, girl.*

A second later, Carmen removed her hand and sat back as well. With the TV on for background noise, the two spent the evening talking. They discussed Joan's music, the state of the world, and celebrities that they each had met. Joan had to beg to hear anything about Carmen's life growing up. All she managed to get out of the woman was one story from her childhood. While Carmen sorted and stacked the picks on the coffee table, she told Joan about the time she and a younger cousin were chased around the kitchen with a wooden spoon for nabbing dessert before its time by her aunt. Carmen hadn't meant for this to nearly turn into an in-home date night, but the intimate setting and the long conversations gave it that feeling by the end.

Only when Joan suggested she that she could fall asleep did Carmen prepare to leave. If Joan was tired, then there was very little chance she would resort to the measures she had the night before. Carmen cleaned up the kitchen, so as not to leave a mess for Joan, before gathering her things so she could head home. Operation Enduring Comfort was a glorious success.

CHAPTER THIRTEEN

Carmen picked Joan up the next day, and they headed for Jerry's office. Everyone was going to meet there, get their equipment loaded, and then board the tour bus for a two-and-a-half-hour drive to Los Angeles. Joan Devintia was scheduled for a 6 p.m. taping of a popular nighttime talk show. She would debut her single in front of a live audience and a multiple-camera set up.

The people in the seats she could handle. It was the ones behind a lens made her nervous. They were watching her, specifically her, exclusively her – waiting for her to rise or fall. Then there was Michael Pearson, a constant man of the hour type with a surprising range of intellect, a knack for comedy, and three golden statuettes for excellence in television. He was ten times the celebrity Joan was. Jerry had to assure his little starlet that she wouldn't be asked anything she wasn't ready for.

When Joan arrived, bodyguard in tow, the office was a whirlwind of activity. While small details were being finalized for the show, Jerry approached. He handed off a list of questions for Joan to review on the bus and suggested that she get herself settled. While Joan went to get her things packed up with the guys, Jerry pulled Carmen aside. He didn't tell her the reason until he was sure that no one else was listening. "Another letter came today, but it didn't go through the mail. It was hand delivered. Nobody seems to know when." He passed over a cream-colored envelope. This time, all that was written on the front was Joan's first name.

Carmen pulled out her gloves and slid them

on so she could take the letter. There was a sense of urgency as she opened it. When people abruptly changed their style, it was usually for the worst if every cop show ever was to be believed.

Inside, she found a recipe for chopped liver and the same smooth penmanship.

I know who that woman is now. The one that's always with you. She's a bodyguard.

Did you think I wouldn't find out? Surely you didn't employ her because of me. I know you didn't. That means someone else has been bothering you. It's all of those pushy photographers, isn't it? Or Mr. Stevenson found out about us, and he's the one that employed her.

No need to worry, my angel. Not even she can keep me from you. I'll make sure of it.

Good luck with your interview tonight.

I'll be watching.

"*Mierda.*" Carmen sighed as she put the letter away.

"What is it?"

Carmen was silent for a moment, thinking over the last sentence she read. "There's a good chance that he's going to be there tonight."

"What?" Jerry pulled at the collar of shirt, suddenly finding it too tight. He lowered his voice, not wanting to draw attention to them. "Do we need to cancel?"

"No. Keep this thing on schedule. We're both going to be with Joan. He's not going to get anywhere near her." Carmen pointed a finger at the manager. "But if I tell you not to leave her side, don't fucking leave her side. Understood?"

Jerry nodded and adjusted his shirt collar once more. This was what he had hired her for and he wasn't about to brush off her expertise.

"Keep cool. Everything stays on schedule," Carmen instructed. "Let's get this over with." Left foot first, Carmen marched Jerry to the bus with confidence. They needed to be at the show's studio well before the six o'clock taping time.

Joan was no stranger to the workings of a tour bus after spending six months on the road with Despite Darkness. She made herself at home on one of the couches and reread a list of questions that the host would ask. Every time she thought she had an acceptable answer for one of them, her mind wandered and the thought escaped. She should have formed a band instead of trying to go it alone, then maybe she wouldn't be doing this interview solo. Then again, she would also have to compete with her bandmates. At least this way she had total creative freedom.

Total freedom to mess this interview up, creatively.

Q: What advice would you give to other musicians that are just starting?

"Don't fuck up."

Carmen looked up from her chair across from Joan. "Huh? Did you say something?"

Joan hadn't realized that she had spoken aloud. "No." She folded the paper in half, then suddenly crumpled it into a ball and chucked it at Rory. He huffed from his mattress and left the trash where it rolled. "No," Joan repeated firmly.

Moving with the unsteady motion of the bus, Carmen walked over to the paper and grabbed it. She opened it back up and worked the worst creases out with her fingers as she read the list. She sat next to Joan and handed the questions back to her. With a knowing smile, she looked at Joan. For a moment, she saw the woman in full combat gear – blonde hair covered by a helmet, bulletproof vest in place of leather jacket, boots instead of heels... Plenty of soldiers were anxious before deployment, herself included.

"If you're not nervous, you're lucky," Carmen said. "If you are nervous... that's normal."

Joan took a deep breath and swallowed. She reached between herself and Carmen, placing her hand in her jacket pocket for a second. When she pulled back, a black and gold pick was resting between her fingers. She showed it off to Carmen and felt her lips upturn into a tempered smile.

"My lucky pick. It came with the first guitar my parents bought me when I was nine. Never do a show without it, bar days included."

146

Carmen dug her fingers into her button up and pulled out a long ball chain. The attached dog tags clinked as they slid from her hand.

"I don't know if they're lucky," she said, shrugging. "But I never take them off."

Joan blinked and had to look away when the metal caught light and reflected it back at her. Carmen always managed to daze her like that.

~*~

Carmen stayed in sight while Joan and the crew did their sound checks and set up. When she wasn't watching Joan, she was marking exits, getting a feel for the layout of the building and the stage, while staring down production interns, the lighting director, and a camera operator or two. No one got past her unnoticed. Arms crossed, Carmen walked over to Jerry and leaned in toward him.

"No Kevin, today?"

Jerry examined his tie before trying to flatten it against his rounded belly. "He took a sick day."

The news coiled her stomach, making Carmen feel a little unwell herself. She couldn't shake the thought that Joan's stalker was someone present in her regular life. Joan's ex was still in prison, but Kevin was everything Joan described. Tall, white, well-dressed, and somewhere Carmen couldn't watch him.

"Keep an eye on her. I'm going to take a look around, see what kind of crowd is waiting to be let in." When he conformed to his newly assigned role, Carmen left.

Outside the studio, ticket-holding guests stretched around the building in a line. Carmen had to wonder how many of them were there because of the host, and how many were there to see Joan. Dark eyes scanned the crowd for a face that she hoped would stand out from the rest. Surely it was easy to spot a psychopath, right?

She did her best to look inconspicuous as she walked past those waiting. It seemed that no one was there alone, and everyone was in good spirits. There was a lot of chatter about the show, several veterans bragging about this being their twenty-something taping, and a lot of selfie activity.

Carmen was about to concede defeat when someone caught her attention. In the center of the line was a tall, lone man in a ball cap that could have been featured in Stalker Weekly. Aside from the shadows on his face, strangeness oozed from his posture and the way the people around him seemed to shun his presence. Even though the line had a single direction: forward – the group behind the man all had their backs turned to him. Carmen narrowed her eyes as she looked the guy over. There was no suit, like Joan described. Only jeans and a baseball jersey. When he suddenly shifted on his feet, she saw the tip of a red tie sticking out of his pocket.

"Son of a bitch," she whispered, darting toward him.

The abrupt activity attracted a few stares from others in the crowd. The ball cap moved up in Carmen's direction. She saw a five o'clock shadow before the man dashed. As he pushed his way out of the line, someone hollered profanities at his dust. Carmen broke into a run after him. A long bus ride wasn't much of a warm up, but adrenaline crashed into her system.

At the first break in buildings, the guy bolted into an alley. Carmen turned the corner to see trashcans knocked over. She jumped the obstacles and had to catch herself from slipping on plastic wrappers. With her stumble, he was gaining ground where she was losing it.

148

When they got back to the street, the stalker almost toppled a couple and sprinted into the road. Having to dodge the same pair, Carmen adjusted her path sooner – costing her precious seconds. By the time she got past the righteously defensive boyfriend, her target was already on the other side of the street. He had successfully managed four lanes of traffic. At forty-five miles an hour, Carmen's chances of achieving the same goal weren't great.

Oh, the things she did for Joan. Like play Frogger with her one life against a fleet of motorists who cursed pedestrians every time they had to stop for one.

Making a mental cross over her chest, Carmen jumped into traffic. She made it through the first three lanes without a hitch or a hospital-worthy injury, but she had misjudged the speed of the coup in the last lane. There wasn't time to stop and stand on a yellow-dotted line, so Carmen leapt onto the hood. The moving force of the vehicle quickly brought her back to the bottom of the windshield. She heard a muffled thump and a crack as she rolled off the other side of coup. Her feet hit the ground and sent pain right to her spine. That stunt hadn't been in basic training, but she had plenty of experience pushing past discomfort and fighting through injuries.

Undeterred, she followed the man to another alley. Before she could catch up to him, he leapt and kicked off the side of a dumpster. He hoisted himself up, losing a piece of his jersey on rusted metal. Carmen was about to follow him when he threw himself at a decrepit ladder. Just as he reached the top rung of the fire escape, the rest of the ladder fell to the pavement. It made an awful screeching noise as the man grunted and pulled himself onto the roof. Carmen wasn't going to be able to follow him. She clenched her fists, breathing hard as he got away.

"Motherfucking parkour," she cursed.

At the base of the dumpster, laughter erupted from a young junkie. Carmen's frustrated stare dropped to a thin woman and the tubing wrapped around her arm. She hadn't asked, but she got Grade-A, white horse advice.

"Can't chase the fellas, honey. Gotta... let'em come to you."

Without another word, the drug user nodded off.

CHAPTER FOURTEEN

Energy in the studio was electric and alive. After a short orientation, the audience had taken their seats. Off set, Joan waited for her cue with the list of questions in her hand. She hadn't seen Carmen since she sat down for hair and makeup. When her direction was given, Joan shoved the paper in a back pocket and strutted onto the stage in a nice selection of fish net, denim, and leather.

Michael Pearson, a man who liked to play pranks on his favorite guests, extended his hand to singer and smiled warmly. Joan locked her jaw when she noticed the scarlet tie wrapped around his neck. He hadn't been wearing that when they met an hour earlier. It wasn't him, though; it wasn't Stan. She swallowed down the panic and waved to the cheering audience. When the host began to speak, the crowd quieted.

"It's a pleasure, Joan. Let me just say, wow. You are stunning."

"Thanks." She took her seat and tried not to think about the thousands of viewers that might watch this when it aired or look down at the triggering fashion accessory. Luckily, the show wasn't live. Anything could be edited out or re-shot as necessary. She was still advised against cursing, but what was a rock star without a few curse words?

Boring, that's what.

"I hope you don't mind if we just dive right into it, because I am excited for you to play. I caught a little during the sound check, and I can't wait for the rest of the world to hear it. I've heard that you've got a pretty tight-knit group of fans from Dodger's. I think a few of them are here." At the bait, a section of the audience shouted and whistled.

Joan looked at the group and smiled. She made out more than a dozen familiar faces and heard Hector shout.

"I love you, Joan!"

That greasy bastard must have had other friends in high places to get a plug like that from Michael Pearson.

"A few of them, huh?" Joan asked, chuckling. "I see some regulars. How are you guys doing?" she said toward the crowd.

"We need beer!" Laughter erupted through the studio.

Michael pushed a customary mug over toward Joan. "Don't tell them, but this is my favorite brew," he whispered more than loud enough for the mics to pick up. After singer and host toasted to the audience's good health with plain water, Michael got to the interview.

"Now, you've got a CD coming out next month, your first, *Snowball Earth*. And I have got to ask, what on Earth does that mean?"

Joan smirked at the first real question. It was one she was expecting even before her manager had given her the list of what Michael might ask. She adjusted herself, leaning on an arm rest so she could get closer to the host before she responded.

"It's the theory that at one point in time the world was completely covered in ice."

Michael raised an eyebrow as he engaged the singer with a rebuttal. "But you're first single is called 'Volcano.'"

"Exactly. Life is very rarely two-sided," Joan explained, coming out of her shell as she gestured with one hand. "People can't live in one extreme or the other. It's a struggle to find the middle ground and

152

exist in a place that's as healthy as it is toxic."

"So it's about balance?"

"Some of it, but there are a couple of fun songs on there, too, like 'Girl Fight.'"

"Speaking of gender, do you expect a lot of trouble working in a male-dominated field?"

Joan shook her head. "Absolutely not. I hope that as a woman I can bring something to different to the table. I want to bring the message that girls can do this. They can do anything they want to. Girls can rock just as hard as the guys, which I'm certainly not the first to say." She was enjoying the chance to speak openly about her music and give her fans a real taste of what she was about on prime-time television.

"Now, you toured with Despite Darkness, whose frontrunner is also female. What can you say about that experience?"

"Only that I loved it. Tanya Rayne was, and is, such a formative influence for me." Joan nailed that answer and she knew it. Her confidence was much improved, and the rest of the interview went by in no time. There were a few more questions about breaking into the industry, inspiration, and plans for the future. Since everything went as planned, Joan had responses for all of them. The host called for a commercial break and made a plug for the new album as the camera moved out into a wide-shot.

Not far, Carmen whispered to herself with a proud smile. "She did it."

Although she had been standing by Jerry the entire time, the man jumped at the sound of her husky voice. "There you are. Did you find anything?"

Carmen shook her head. She had chased off the suspicious guy – and that knowledge was reserved for her alone. The less people that knew, the less chance Joan had of figuring it out.

After the main interview, everything was set

up for the performance. When the band played, Carmen realized she was humming along to the first verse. Joan had an astounding voice, and the music was starting to grow on her.

When the set ended, Carmen turned to Jerry. "No autographs tonight, all right? Make up some excuse." The junkie's words about letting guys come to her was still floating around her head. The man could have come back, and Carmen wasn't sure she could do another chase.

The manager headed off to find his singer, already coming up with a reason to get her straight onto the bus. Carmen waited by the door, glancing out to make sure no one was hanging out by the vehicle. She watched Joan lead the entourage away from the studio, a disappointed look on her face and an unused marker hanging on her shirt. She didn't know what excuse Jerry had given Joan, but they did have another busy day tomorrow and a second road trip in front of them.

Carmen waited patiently, and then fell in step beside Joan as they headed out to the bus.

"You sure this was your first interview?" she questioned with a grin. "You did great."

"It wasn't my first if you count the interview for ROCK 105.3, or the magazine Audio Wonder, or the one time my elementary classmates did an exposé on the food from the cafeteria." Joan laughed at herself. Carmen had quite the calming effect on her after all the time they spent together the night before. She was glad to know that Carmen had been around for her interview, even if she did disappear during the prep.

Carmen snickered as she let Joan get onto the bus first. "I'm sure that one in elementary was absolutely riveting."

After twenty minutes of driving, Joan was ready to lay down. Unfortunately, there were only two bunks on this bus. Tony was asleep in one; Rory was laying in the other, lightly – but still obnoxiously – playing his guitar and fiddling with the same chord over and over. Joan's options were very limited. If she *had* to choose between the floor and half of a couch because Carmen was sitting at one end, she'd pick the couch. And, well, she *did* have to choose.

Without saying what she was up to, Joan rested her head beside Carmen and laid on her back, leaving her legs up and bent at the knee. It wasn't the most incredibly comfortable position.

Pleading, blue eyes glanced up at Carmen. "Do you mind if I rest my head on your lap?"

Trying to look very unamused, Carmen stared down at Joan. "Let's see... I'm your bodyguard, personal trainer, chef, and now a traveling pillow? This list is starting to get pretty long, Ms. Devintia," she teased. As she spoke, she got herself as comfortable as she could. Her back was screaming at her not to move, but she wouldn't worry about it until she got home. "Yeah, go ahead."

Joan smiled as she got what she wanted. She positioned her head onto one of the woman's legs and held back a complaint about how muscle didn't make the best traveling pillow.

"You're as useful as a Swiss Army knife- or a Swiss Marine... knife..." Joan faltered, realizing how ridiculous she sounded. She pursed her lips and cut Carmen off before she could reply. "Shut up." She whined at herself and closed her eyes.

Carmen laughed silently and tried not to grimace at the pain it caused her. "Calm down," she soothed Joan, placing a hand on the woman's shoulder. "Get some rest."

Joan took a few deep breaths through her nose with a grin tugging at the corner of her mouth. It wasn't pitch black in the luxury vehicle, but it was pleasantly dark with the lights dimmed. Carmen was warm, and it dawned on Joan how much she missed being physically close to someone.

She planned to enjoy it, knowing Carmen probably wouldn't have let just anyone rest on her like this. They had a connection, didn't they? Weren't they friends? Or was she just fooling herself and wishfully thinking that money wasn't the only thing keeping Carmen around...

CHAPTER FIFTEEN

Sitting outside the Marmax building all day would have been uncomfortable for anyone less worthy. It didn't bother him, though. After yesterday's ruined attempt to see Joan at the taping of her interview, his mind had fixated on the need to see her some other way. He wasn't going to be chased away again. All he had to do was wait until she was alone.

It was a shame that car hadn't flattened Joan's guard dog.

When he finally saw the bodyguard leave the Marmax building, he slouched down in his seat and waited for the SUV to pull away. She had stayed with Joan for a long time… longer than he would have liked. To be safe, he stayed where he was and watched the moon ascend between high-rise buildings.

It was nearing three in the morning when the moon disappeared behind a tall plaza of orange lights and he finally got out of his car. He reached up and pulled the hood over his head as he walked to the hotel. His first obstacle was getting past security, but that proved not to be an obstacle at all thanks to the gossip magazine in the guard's hands. He got through the lobby and to the private elevator, using the keycard he'd acquired to access it. The woman sitting at the security desk didn't so much as give him a second glance.

After the ride to the penthouse level, he stepped out of the elevator. He could hear his heartbeat pounding in his ears – he was close. So close. His thoughts tried to run away with him, but he remained grounded in the fact that in just moments he would see Joan.

The key in his sweaty fingers slid effortlessly into the door and he pushed it open. He hesitated just long enough to adjust his tie before he broke the threshold with a quiet step. Inside the penthouse, he saw that the TV was still on – providing plenty of background noise to cover his presence and light to navigate the foreign space.

He looked around as he moved further in, barely able to remember to breathe as he walked. His fingertips ran over the back of the couch, and he inhaled deeply. The space smelled like her – he would never forget. He paused at the saltwater tank and flipped on the light to see the fish inside. Little Sunshine and his fellow seahorses startled awake. Instead of dancing for their food, a couple of them readjusted the grip on their hitches. They floated peacefully behind the protective glass while he watched them.

In the corner of his eye, he caught sight of the bedroom door. It was open, and Joan was in that room.

Slowly, with measured steps, he approached. The light behind him cast long shadows, but he could still see the form in the bed. It took every ounce of self-control he had not to go to her then and there. She would be so happy to see him. They'd both been waiting so long already…

He had to wait for the right time, though. For now, he had to settle for this.

He stayed by the door, watching Joan sleep for a long time. The thought of getting closer crossed his mind, but he didn't want to wake her. She was so serene, so beautiful. Unbidden, he felt a wet trail on his cheek and he nearly choked on an inhale of air. Quickly, he reached up and scraped away the tears, leaving his skin to burn with light scratches.

158

Joan's beauty, just her *being*, was enough to make him weep like a child.

Eventually, he knew he needed to leave. If he stayed much longer, there was the risk that she would wake and see him there. He crept further into the room and carefully laid a rose and a note on the bedside stand.

The words were short and sweet, straight to the point: *You're beautiful when you sleep, my angel.*

Before moving away from the bed, his gaze dropped to the woman laying down not even a foot from him. He turned and reached out, his fingertips just barely an inch from touching her. Rather than making contact, he pulled his hand away and turned around.

On his way out of the penthouse, he saw a shirt that was lying out, so he grabbed it and left.

~*~

Early in the morning, Joan's alarm went off with an hour to spare before she had to be out of the door for the final day of shooting her music video. She rolled over, silenced the iPhone, and then jerked her hand back in pain. A bright red bubble sat on the tip of her pointer finger. She had pricked herself on the thorn of a rose. Confused, she grabbed a tissue from the nightstand and wiped away the blood while she stared at the flower.

Her first, sleepy impression was to be happy for the gift Carmen had given her, but that couldn't be right. She remembered Carmen leaving. Hell, she was with the woman practically from sun up until past sun down. Carmen never left a flower, of all foolish things, in that time. She walked out on amiable terms of course, but nothing more. Nothing like a cherry red rose would suggest.

Joan squeezed the tissue to the cut when she noticed a piece of paper under the dying plant. She recognized her handwriting. The note was from her binge-induced writing session, but it was folded down the middle. After sweeping her hair away from her undercut, she reached for the paper and turned the inside toward her face.

A peaceful morning shattered. She dropped the note and lunged for her phone. She pulled the device back as if she were tugging her hand from a live bear trap. The teeth had already grazed her skin once. With no memory of how she got there, Joan locked herself in the bathroom. She slumped against the tub and wrapped an arm around her legs to keep them from shaking. Facing the door and watching the knob for any signs of movement, Joan called the only safety she knew.

Carmen had been up since six, and she was on her way home from the gym. She had cut it a bit shorter than usual, tired from her late night with Joan and not wanting to overdo it. Her back still ached after being hit by the coup. With a groan, Carmen settled into the seat of her SUV. Just as she started the engine, she saw her cell light up and lifted an eyebrow. It was early for Joan to be calling.

"Hello?" Carmen answered.

Joan's head shot up from her knees when she heard Carmen's raspy voice. "He was here- He still might be!" She knew she had to speak clearly, but it was hard to slow down. "There was a note next to my bed when I woke up."

Carmen immediately put her car into drive. "Okay, okay," she tried to soothe. "I'm not far. Are you somewhere safe?"

"I locked myself in the bathroom." If Joan's stalker was still around, it was the safest place she could be since the door didn't unlock from the other

160

side. In the emptiness between sentences, Joan kept expecting to hear banging on the door and an angry voice that sounded a lot like her ex.

"Good," Carmen said. "Just hang on for a few minutes, okay? I'll be right there. Don't leave the bathroom, don't unlock the door until I get there. It's going to be all right." She pressed the gas pedal down, pushing her car past what was legal just to get to Joan as quickly as she could.

Joan put her head back down as she listened to Carmen's voice. Her backside was growing cold against the porcelain, and her feet were already numb. A thin Raiders jersey was her only protection from the cold. It wasn't enough. The locks to her apartment weren't enough. A bodyguard wasn't enough. How could she be doing this again? How could she have put a lock between herself and the rest of her life a second time? She was a prisoner of her own fame and the attention it brought.

Stan was doing this to torture her. He'd come to her penthouse last night and let her sleep in his presence, just to prove that he could have her whenever he wanted. There was no place safe for her. Joan fought panic with a singular thought. She wasn't alone in this nightmare; Carmen was on her way.

A frustrated sigh left Carmen when she came to a red light – it was the last one before the Marmax building. When it turned green, the cars in front of her weren't getting up to speed fast enough.

"*Ay, Dios mío,*" she swore vehemently, but didn't raise her voice. "*Mierda de cabeza. Sale de la manera, pinche gringo.*"

Joan had heard Carmen speak and curse in Spanish before, on the rare occasion that the bodyguard was frustrated about something. It usually amused her even though she didn't understand it. No smile graced her pale lips this time.

161

When Carmen finally got to the building, she jumped out of the SUV – ignoring the discomfort it caused her. "Joan, I'm coming up right now," she promised. "I'll probably lose service in the elevator, but I'm on my way. Just take slow breaths. I'll be there in less than-" Carmen stopped talking when she heard her phone beep. She had lost the call.

The ride up seemed to take longer than it usually did, but once the doors began to divide, she shoved herself through them. She jogged down the short hall and retrieved the gun from her waistband. After opening the door, she swept the immediate area. When she didn't see anyone, she called out to the rocker.

"Joan! Stay where you're at! I'm coming to you!" She had to examine each room before going to the bathroom. Handgun lifted and finger resting on the trigger guard, Carmen did a thorough search of the place. Instead of flashing back to a warzone, she remembered the day before. In the living room, Joan had showed off her rock-heavy vinyl collection. In the kitchen, they argued over the best way to make grilled cheese – obviously *without* tomato. In Joan's bedroom, they shared a moment when Carmen asked Joan to play her favorite song when she was growing up. The song was over too quickly, and Joan's teasing after was deadly. So what if Carmen liked *one* boy band? She had been sixteen once.

Certain that they were alone, Carmen put away her gun and walked over to the bathroom. "Open the door, Joan. It's okay."

Joan was slow to stand. On bare feet, she stepped up to door and turned the lock with trembling fingers. Some rocker she turned out to be, huh? What kick-ass bitch hides in a bathroom? She opened the door and stared at Carmen. One glance into the other woman's eyes and she saw how serious this was. As

162

Carmen looked her over for injuries, Joan felt sympathy pain in her teeth for how tight Carmen's jaw was.

"Are you okay?" Carmen finally managed to ask. How could Joan be okay? They were facing a man resourceful enough to get an unlisted number and acquire access to the Marmax penthouse. He was psychotic enough to think he was secretly dating a woman he had never met. And he was cunning enough to slip right past her at every turn. An intruder had been inside the penthouse, extremely close to Joan – she was surprised and relieved all at once that nothing more serious had happened.

Carmen watched Joan flounder at the question. The singer's lips opened and shut with the smallest sounds before Joan stepped in. When Joan's head dropped onto her shoulder, Carmen wrapped her arms around her. A second later, Joan's fingers dug into her shirt and her heart clenched.

"I've got you now. You're safe."

Joan's face warmed as her eyes welled with tears. She didn't mean to cry; she didn't mean to babble.

"He was here. He was right here in my room, watching me sleep, and I didn't even know."

Joan didn't know what to do now, but she couldn't stay in her apartment until the locks were changed and a deadbolt or ten were installed. She couldn't even focus on taking care of that; she had to get ready to go the studio. There was a video to finish today.

"He's not here now," Carmen told her. "I'll talk to the guys at the security desk, have them switch out locks on your door. He won't get in again." There could be a day or two delay when maintenance was involved, depending on how the situation was handled. In that time, they would have to find a place for Joan to stay that was safer.

Gradually, Joan uncurled her fingers from around the black shirt and took a step back. After wiping her tired eyes, she folded her arms over herself and glanced at the nightstand. Joan never felt more uncomfortable in her own apartment than right now. She nodded at the short furniture and whispered.

"He left that."

Carmen nodded and walked over to the nightstand, checking out the rose and the note without touching them. She pulled out her phone and brought up Sam's number. This was a criminal investigation now.

"Sam, I need you to come to the Marmax building," Carmen explained when the man answered. "The guy broke in last night... No, she's fine... He left another note and a flower... All right, see you soon." After pocketing the phone, she turned back to Joan. "Go ahead and get dressed. We're not going anywhere for a while. I'll call Jerry and let him know the shoot needs to be postponed."

Joan went to her dresser and retrieved a pair of washed out jeans. "We can't postpone the video. I can't," she clarified. She stepped into the denim, unconcerned that the bodyguard was still in the room with her. What bothered her was the fact that Carmen's cop-buddy was coming to her apartment. "I can't let him keep me from living my life."

"Joan, this just turned into a crime scene. We can't leave right now." Carmen averted her gaze, at first. "Sam won't take long." Curiosity lifted her eyes and she followed the jeans as they moved up the woman's thighs. "We'll be in the studio later... this... morning." When Joan pulled off her jersey, she quickly looked away again.

164

"Fine," Joan surrendered. Shut down, she set her shirt on top of the dresser and retrieved a bra. When Carmen walked away a second later, Joan pursed her lips and looked down at herself. She needed to make the time to get another tattoo.

While Carmen was in the living room on the phone with Jerry, Joan used the distraction to remove the illegal drugs from her bedroom and put them in her purse. She couldn't leave them around for some cop to find, even if that cop was Carmen's friend. The gossip magazines were quick enough to assume drug use; the rock star didn't need to prove them right. Even if it was just recreational...

The call to Jerry took longer than Carmen would have liked. Though he understood the situation, the manager was still upset that production was on hold. Of all the times for their troublemaker to cause a problem... but he agreed to stall until that afternoon, so that Carmen could take care of Joan and the police.

Twenty minutes after Carmen got off the phone, there was a knock on the door. Still cautious, the bodyguard went to check it out, looking through the peephole and finding her friend waiting on the other side. She opened the door and let the man inside. He was dressed in business casual clothes, rather than a police uniform.

"Just you?" she questioned, not seeing anyone else behind him.

Sam nodded. "Yeah. The less police presence, the better for these cases."

Carmen was relieved as she brought the officer in to meet the rocker. "Joan, this is Sam Macrae," she introduced them.

Sam took a step forward and offered his hand as he spoke. "Ms. Devintia. I'm sorry we have to meet under these kind of conditions."

165

Joan nodded at the officer as she shook his hand. He was a big guy, big enough to look six feet from a distance. With the power of the law on his side, he had the right connections to obtain unlisted numbers. He could have coerced security to get him access to the top floor. He would know Carmen was Joan's bodyguard, and he had the evidence of Stan's letters to destroy or tamper with as he pleased... but he was also black.

She managed to smile at him, thankful that she didn't need to be paranoid that he could be Stan.

Sam politely smiled back before he glanced at Carmen. "So, there was a letter and flower?"

Carmen showed him into Joan's bedroom. "On the nightstand," she said, pointing to the evidence. "Might actually get prints off of it this time... Do you think he'd remember gloves?"

"He might not have," Sam answered. He produced a pair of gloves and an evidence bag from his pocket. After reading the message he shook his head and slid it into the bag, along with the flower. "I'll take these back to the station with me, have them both checked for prints. I want to find the pen he wrote with, too. Get looking, Savedra."

Carmen quirked a brow at the man. "That sounded a lot like an order," she muttered to herself as she scanned the immediate area.

This was what Joan had feared. She watched Carmen and Sam conquer and divide. They tried not to disturb too much as they hunted for the pen. Instead of looking, Joan walked out to her seahorses. In the madness of the morning, she had forgotten to care for them.

When she saw that the aquarium light was already on, she flared her nostrils. She didn't remember leaving it on.

166

"Sorry, kiddos," she whispered. As she fed the fish, the hunt for the pen came to the rest of the penthouse.

Eventually, Sam gave up to examine the front door and called Carmen off the search after failing to find a single rollerball pen. "He must have taken it with him. There's no sign of forced entry on the door."

"Apparently, he has resources." Carmen shrugged. "He had an unlisted number that he called from. Maybe he paid somebody off for a key, or maybe he works here, but my background checks on the staff didn't really turn up anything."

Sam looked over at Joan. "Who has access to this floor?"

"Carmen has my only spare key, but the staff can get up here. Jerry," she paused to think who else. "And the man who owns the building... When I'm on the road, a guy from the cleaning crew comes in to take care of my aquarium."

Sam pulled out a notepad and a pen from his shirt pocket. "I need his name and all the contact information you have."

"But Isaiah-"

"Ms. Devintia," Sam interrupted. "I know fame has a large role to play, but we can't ignore the people you know and trust." He handed over the pad for Joan to write on and waited patiently until it was returned to him. "I recommend staying elsewhere for a few days, if not until we catch him."

Joan glanced at Carmen when the officer recommended living somewhere else. Her mind knew what it wanted, but her good sense had other ideas.

"I can get a hotel room, or stay with one of my bandmates," she said. Rory and Bruce would take her in if she told them what was going on. Hell, they were just as likely to try and catch the stalker themselves, Rory especially. That was part of the reason she hadn't told them.

Carmen shook her head at Joan's suggestions. A hotel was just like her penthouse – the stalker could get in with little problem. And her bandmates... Carmen figured they would binge on drugs and alcohol if in that situation. That wasn't something Joan needed right now.

"Those places really aren't that safe," she pointed out. "You can stay with me if you want." Her apartment wasn't very big, but it would be adequate for the two of them. She'd give Joan her bed and sleep on the couch herself. She could keep a close eye on Joan that way, too.

Joan raised an eyebrow Carmen, almost breaking into a smile. Almost.

"So, now you're my landlord, too?" she said under her breath. The comment was for the other woman only.

She wanted to be with Carmen, but not like this.

"The list just keeps growing," Carmen agreed quietly.

Sam put the notepad back into his pocket and went to grab the evidence bag. "I'll escort you both out today, then I'm going to check with security," he told the two women. "We're keeping this case as quiet as possible during the investigation, but once we catch this guy... arrests and charges are public record. The media will find out."

Joan sighed; that wasn't what she wanted to hear. But she wasn't the first celebrity to file charges against a stalker, and she wouldn't be the last. The press would forget in a week, or however quickly the next big story broke. Maybe Joan would get lucky, and one of the popular boy groups would split up.

"Guess I'll pack before we go then," Joan

commented. She found a piece of luggage in a closet and almost called the whole staying-with-Carmen thing off. It was her brown, heavyweight suitcase – the one she left David's with. And here she was, packing it again for the exact opposite reason. She wasn't standing up to her terrorist, she was running from him. "Damn it," she cursed to herself.

As she grabbed her clothes, she realized that she couldn't find one of her favorite shirts. Her penthouse wasn't the most organized suite in the building. She had left it out for the simple fact that she had planned on wearing it the day before, changed her mind, and didn't put it away.

"He took something," Joan announced to the room. "He took one of my shirts." That confession creeped her out. God only knew what Stan wanted it for.

Carmen knit her eyebrows together. "Are you sure?"

"Yeah, I'm sure." Joan scratched the back of her neck, trying to dispel some rampant nerves. The more she thought about the situation, the more it angered her. "What's he fucking waiting for?" She turned to Sam, figuring he would know more about criminal motivation than Carmen. "It's been two months with this shit. He shows up outside of restaurants, at parties, in my own apartment..." Joan's message was clear. Stan could have hurt her last night. He had all the opportunity in the world, but he didn't. "What's he waiting for?"

Sam took a deep breath. "Motive is never one-size-fits-all. He could have a specific date or scenario in mind. Or he could just be biding his time. We won't know for sure until we have him in handcuffs, and even then... we might not know."

Joan was silent for a minute as she finished packing and let Sam's words sink in. She thanked the officer for his discretion and told Carmen that she was ready to go. They would still have to go back to the penthouse to feed her fish if that was something she couldn't trust Isaiah with anymore.

CHAPTER SIXTEEN

The day on set was a flash for Joan. She threw herself into the shoot, giving the director everything he needed to finish the video and apologized profusely for keeping the crew waiting. That left one more day in the recording studio to finish *Snowball Earth* before Jerry had to get the music to the production team so the CDs could be made. They were right on time, despite all the bumps in the road.

On the way to Carmen's place, Joan wondered what she would find. She knew Carmen liked things precise. It was in the way Carmen always ate her food clockwise if it was on a plate. With the soldier's history, she expected bolts on the doors. Carmen also enjoyed fantasy and sci-fi movies, so maybe she would have a case of DVD's – shelves lined with all the major sets: *Star Wars, The Lord of the Rings, Pirates of the Caribbean...*

When they got to the building, Carmen took a deep breath to calm her nerves. She'd entertained the thought of having Joan over, but now that it was actually here – well, there was a reason her hands were getting a bit sweaty as she singled out the right key. This was her personal sanctuary; this was a massive step for her.

She led Joan into the beige building and up a single flight of concrete stairs. Her one-bedroom apartment was one the second floor, making trips to the grocery store a mini workout. She could have afforded something nicer, but she found comfort in scuffed walls, fading graffiti tags, and weeds growing from the sidewalk. She took a left down the hall and went all the way down to the last door on the right.

"It's not a penthouse, but here we are," she said, unlocking the door and holding it for Joan.

The clean apartment had only two prerequisites for furniture: everything had to be dark in color, and if someone was going to sit on it, it had to be comfortable. The living room housed a couch, coffee table, and a large entertainment center that held a decently sized TV and her movie collection. There was one bedroom, with a full size bed, nightstand, and dresser in it.

After Joan walked inside, Carmen closed the door. She methodically locked up like she did every time she came home.

Doorknob.

Deadbolt.

Chain.

Joan's lips upturned as she watched Carmen's practiced routine. No solid brass chain or lock made her feel as safe as knowing Carmen would be with her all night. It was true, the apartment was about the quarter of the size of her penthouse, but despite a lack of decor it felt more intimate, more like a place that was lived in instead of Joan's constant whirlwind of being in and out.

"I'm sorry to intrude like this." Joan knew it wasn't really her fault, but she felt as though she was putting Carmen in a bad spot.

Carmen visually double-checked the door, before turning away from it. "You're not intruding," she argued. It certainly wasn't Joan's fault that she couldn't stay in her penthouse. "Make yourself at home."

Carmen strode through the living room and went out into the kitchen to empty her pockets. She put each item on the counter and, tight-lipped as ever, shifted them until they lined up perfectly. She could have tried to be a little less compulsive, but she already knew it wouldn't work.

Joan grimaced to herself as she watched Carmen's OCD take center stage. She wasn't sure she could make herself at home here; she wasn't sure she should. What if she rested her suitcase against the wrong wall or moved something out of place when she walked by it? She was very serious about being a good guest and friend.

When Carmen finished, she returned to the living room. "You can take my bed," she told Joan – who had yet to move from her place by the door. "I'll sleep on the couch."

Joan readjusted her grip on the handle of her suitcase but tilted her head to the side. "Are you sure? I promise I'm not too delicate for a couple of nights on a couch." She didn't want to displace Carmen.

Carmen offered Joan a smile. "I'm sure. You go ahead." Her mother had taught her to accommodate her guests before herself.

"All right." Joan took her suitcase into the bedroom. Maybe she'd questioned the other woman for the sole fact that Joan didn't take to sleeping in other people's beds – unless those individuals were also present.

Quietly, trying not to disturb things, she set the luggage on the end of the mattress. She lingered for a moment, glancing around the room. From the black-out curtains to the sheets, everything was black or some variation thereof. There was a standalone, full-length mirror next to an open closet. She made out the square-patterned camouflage of military uniforms inside, but aside from that, there was nothing else visible in the bedroom that suggested military service... Except for the stark fact that everything seemed to be spotless and organized in a certain manner. As for the rest of the closet, clothes were arranged by color, then length of fabric. It was controlled and intense.

Joan rubbed the tattoo on her shoulder when it dawned on her that Carmen had taken a big risk inviting her back here. Carmen had organized and cleaned her way into a haven of predictability and authority. But Joan was an unknown factor, a loose cannon of sorts. Nothing about her was good for Carmen.

Smiley-face under her thumb, Joan sighed and retreated from her thoughts. She found her host on the couch and joined her. It wasn't late enough to retire yet, so Joan took more thorough look around.

There were only a few pictures in the apartment, and all of them were set up on the entertainment center. One was of a brooding teen enveloped by a pair of smiling adults on graduation day: High School Edition. Another photograph was a colorful portrayal of the Virgin Mary. The last one was of a squad of Marines while on deployment, out in the desert – likely the Middle East.

Beside Joan, Carmen was settling a bit as she examined the TV guide for something to watch. The world hadn't ended when Joan entered the space, and everything was turning out to be all right. Besides, she could clean when her company was gone if it was necessary. There was nothing that could be done that wouldn't be able to be fixed. After settling on a campy Hollywood flick, she glanced at Joan.

"If you're hungry, I can make us something or we can order out."

Joan's attention drifted from the television while Carmen spoke. It didn't matter to her what they ate, but after not eating much because of stress, she was starving.

"It's up to you, personal chef." She gave Carmen a playful smile.

"I'll make us something," Carmen decided. She handed the TV remote to Joan before she got up and went into the kitchen. She started putting a quick dinner together for the two of them. It was strange to make food for more than just herself in her home, but she adjusted. The night's menu consisted of shredded beef tacos and homemade salsa shipped from Columbus, Ohio. Written in marker on top of the aluminum lid was the current year and her family name. Back home, her mother spent days canning salsa. As a kid, Carmen was always ready to help with her favorite part: sampling.

Since Carmen didn't have the room for a kitchen table, the two of them ate on the couch. After dinner, it was too late in the evening to find any good television except for a few talk shows that Joan couldn't care enough to be interested in. Instead of worrying about finding something to watch, Joan lowered the volume of the TV, sat back against the leather couch, and closed her eyes.

She listened to Carmen wash dishes by hand and wondered what her parents would think of her for not helping. She had tried. Carmen answered her, "I'll help you," with a humble, "Relax. You've had a long day." That was true. It was a gloriously soothing feeling to know she could shut her eyes and still be safe.

A few minutes passed before Joan looked through the living room again. She'd seen the pictures on the entertainment system, but she had missed the small, black container next to the photograph of Carmen's squad. There was a medal inside, Joan realized. A Purple Heart, awarded to soldiers injured in war. Had Carmen been hurt? Of all the visible scars on Carmen, Joan couldn't say any of them looked out of the ordinary. Maybe she'd find the courage to ask, or maybe she would let sleeping dogs lie.

About twenty minutes later, Carmen returned to the living room. She resumed her seat on the couch, a little closer to Joan this time.

"If you're tired, you can go on to bed," she offered.

Joan frowned. "I don't know if I can sleep." Sure, she could close her eyes for a few minutes here and there, but falling asleep... The prospect wasn't appealing. She could use a distraction and began to run her fingers through her hair.

When she spoke again, her voice cracked. "That's... a Purple Heart, isn't it?"

Carmen glanced up at the object in question and nodded. Had she known it was going to be a conversation-starter, she would have put it away. She couldn't fault Joan for being curious and prepared herself to explain. Somewhere packed in a closet was a letter from the Medical Evaluation Board. They were so cut-and-dry about her medical condition, but she didn't think she could pull that off with Joan. Joan made her heart beat faster.

"How... um. How did you get it?"

Taking a long breath, Carmen looked away from Joan. Where Joan's social circle was the sun, she was content with the moon. Very few people knew about her Purple Heart, and once she told Joan there would be another moon landing. Once she told Joan, Joan was in.

Carmen glanced downward, picking at some invisible speck on her dark jeans. "We were on the last mission of our deployment – one more damn week and we were going to be at a ski resort, like we'd promised each other. My squad was out on recon, and we had just finished checking a position for hostile forces. On our way back to base, we were bullshitting – talking about strip clubs and the end of deployment..." She leaned forward and set her elbows

176

on her knees for a moment. The pause lasted too long, and she lost the resolve to continue until she looked at Joan. The woman was beautiful, undercut and all.

"There was an IED on the road, and we hit it. It tore apart the passenger side of our Humvee, flipped us over. Sam lost his leg that day, and I brought home these."

As she finished speaking, Carmen shifted in her seat again. She grabbed the hem of her shirt and the waistband of her pants to move them out of the way. A five-inch-long scar ran from her hip up toward her stomach as a diagonal testament to what a person can survive. There was a shorter scar, a couple of inches lower. Much further down, she had a patchwork of scars on her thigh, but that remained hidden under her clothes.

"Half the squad died that day," Carmen added, pulling her clothing back into its proper place. "The rest of us were stabilized on base, then we were sent to a hospital in Germany to recover."

Joan swallowed and let her hand fall between them. She had stopped fiddling with her hair some time ago.

"Did you guys still go skiing?" she asked.

Carmen faintly shook her head. "No... After everything that happened, none of us were in shape to." Some of them weren't hurt as badly as others, but they all had to spend time in the hospital. With staggered release dates, a devastating memorial to attend, and rehabilitation, no one had the time or energy to schedule in the promise. It was such a devastating loss, but they pulled through it together.

After a moment's uncertainty, Joan's hand crossed the marked inches between them. She placed her palm over Carmen's hand and slowly curled her fingers around the other woman's.

Carmen's own indecision kept her from doing anything right away. Her fight-or-flight instinct was making her tense up as she zeroed in on her nearest exit: a hasty retreat to her kitchen. She maintained enough control to keep from pulling her hand away, though. What good would it do for her to struggle against the comfort Joan was offering? How would it help her to run? Instead, she turned her hand over in Joan's and entwined their fingers. One small step for Joan; one giant leap for Carmen.

For a second there, Joan had to wonder if she'd made a mistake. When Carmen finally reacted, Joan smiled at her and rubbed her thumb back and forth over tan skin.

"What will you do?" Joan asked, happy to break the silence and change the subject. "When you don't have to protect me anymore?" she clarified. She didn't want to leave the soldier behind on the battlefield, so she chose to talk about the future. It was Joan's impression that Carmen was hired on until Stan was dealt with. Otherwise, bodyguards could come and go as she needed for certain public events.

Carmen looked down at their joined hands. Joan was the first person besides Sam and her family to touch her without severe repercussions. Certainly that had to mean something.

"I haven't decided yet," she answered honestly. She was so invested lately that thoughts of what was to come after had been put from her mind. Truth be told, she didn't want to leave Joan once this was all taken care of.

"You wouldn't just guard someone else?" Joan's serious question fell to teasing. "Oh, God- I've ruined you for guarding. I mean, I know I'm difficult but..."

Carmen smirked before she offered a shrug. "Maybe," she told Joan, glancing over at the other

178

woman. Her smile grew just looking at Joan. If this was 'ruined' then at least the wrecking ball came with compassion and one hell of a view.

Since Carmen seemed to be feeling better, Joan took her hand back and sat up. The two talked into the night on various subjects, but out of mutual respect the conversation was kept light.

Around 11 PM Joan yawned twice in the same minute, and Carmen totally busted her for it.

"I'm getting ready for bed," Carmen announced. "You should do the same… Unless you plan on returning the favor, and you're going to sit out here as my personal pillow all night."

Joan hummed for a moment as if she were actually considering it. "That sounds like too much work for a celeb like me," she answered, putting a hand over her chest. Carmen rolled her eyes as she walked away.

Joan let Carmen have access to the bedroom and bathroom first, then changed into the pajamas she brought. Before Carmen could get too comfortable on the couch, she wandered into the living room in her Raiders jersey and cotton pants with cartoon robots on them. For fear that Carmen would laugh at her own apparel, she didn't dare say a word about Carmen's skull-covered boxers. But she hadn't come to check out what Carmen was wearing even if she was into women in tank tops.

"Will you wake me up when you get up?" she finally asked. Joan didn't know what time that would be, but since she was living with Carmen she would go by the other woman's schedule.

"You wouldn't know what to do with yourself if you got up at the same time as me," Carmen teased. She pulled a blanket off the back of the couch and caught sight of Joan crossing her arms over her chest with a smirk.

"Fine. Then I'll be up at seven." A thought came to mind, and Joan softened her posture. "Are you gonna leave me behind while you go to the gym?" She wasn't keen on being left alone after what happened this morning, but she knew that Carmen had a schedule and preferred to stick to it.

"I'm actually going to skip the gym," Carmen answered.

Joan nodded. "Then take a page out of my book and sleep in," she suggested with a grin. She turned and bid Carmen farewell over her shoulder. "Have a good night."

"You too," Carmen said, watching Joan walk off. "I'll be right out here if you need anything… Sleep well in your robot pajamas!"

Joan spun around, disbelief clearly written on her features. "Oh, I will," she baited. "But skull boxers? How incredibly butch of you."

Carmen laughed as she spread the blanket out. "The ladies like it."

Joan bit her tongue. Busted again. This was not how she imagined her night would go. She turned back around and retreated, wearing a new shade of red.

In the bedroom, she familiarized herself with the space one more time before she shut off the light. With a flip of a switch, the room was thrown into darkness. Joan didn't let her eyes adjust; she just moved forward. The bed was probably about five, maybe six-

"Ow! Mother-fuck!" She turned just enough to plop onto the mattress so she could hold her aching shin.

Carmen's stern voice pierced the walls between them. "You all right?"

Cheeks warming again, Joan sat up straight and hollered back. "I'm fine!" She leaned back,
180

whining to herself as gravity helped her into bed. Such grace, such beauty, such fucking embarrassment.

Joan pulled herself onto the rest of the mattress and moved the covers out of her way so she could lie properly. Carmen's bed was more comfortable than she imagined it would be. But, maybe, after years of sleeping on cots that were comparable to plywood, Carmen wanted something softer.

Joan settled herself and closed her eyes. It was weird trying to sleep without some kind of white noise in the background. In place of a television or a fan, her mind kept her occupied with a bombardment of thoughts. Amidst the chaos of half-formed curiosities and foggy plans, two thoughts stood out in particular. She was spending the night in Carmen's bed. And Carmen wasn't in it with her.

CHAPTER SEVENTEEN

Joan's night was a bit restless. She had woken up so many times that she couldn't be sure how much sleep she got. The door between the bedroom and the rest of the apartment was thick enough to block the noise of Carmen making breakfast, but once the air conditioning kicked on, Joan smelled the undeniable scent of bacon.

She still had twenty minutes before her alarm went off, but there was no debate to stay in bed. She made a quick stop to the bathroom and assured herself that she didn't look too terrible before she joined Carmen in the small kitchen. She was still absolutely rocking her robot pajamas as well as a new bruise on her leg. Shame be damned.

"Morning," she greeted with a lazy grin.

Carmen glanced up from stirring a pan of eggs when Joan spoke, offering the woman a smile. "Good morning. I hope you like omelets."

"I'm into them." Joan went toward the cabinets and found the one the cups were in on the first try. "And robots," she added. "And skull boxers." She heard the spatula handle hit the side of the pan behind her and tried not to laugh. Carmen must have dropped it.

"Good to know," Carmen rasped.

With coffee, breakfast, and cheerful company, Joan's morning was much better than the last. The pair left for the recording studio on time, but Joan was feeling a bit wistful that it was her last day to get what she needed to finish the CD. Halfway there, her new cell phone rang, alerting her to a text from Jerry.

Turn on 105.3, rock star.

Joan bit her lip and turned toward Carmen. "Mind if I change the station for a minute?"

Carmen took her eyes off the road for just a moment to glance at Joan. "Go ahead."

Joan hit seek until the bright green numbers of Carmen's radio read: 105.3. The audio of the normal morning disc-jockey picked up less than half a second later.

"-ridiculous amount of requests for this new single. Not that I blame any of you. If you haven't heard it yet, well, you're about to. This is Joan Devintia with 'Volcano.'"

"Molten rage moves up slowly
Still don't know what sets you off
I just taste fire, I feel the flame
You could try to hurt me, but I feel no pain"

Joan swallowed nervously before she was taken host by a glorious smile. She had heard a couple songs from her EP on some indie and college stations; she had a few small deals with radio streaming services, and she was featured by 105.3 a couple of months ago. But this was something entirely different. Blue eyes darted from the radio to Carmen.

She spoke over herself – quite a strange a feat, she had to admit. "You must be sick of this song," she joked, trying not to feel her growing vanity. She reached to change the station back, happy enough that Jerry had given her opportunity to catch "Volcano" on the mainstream airwaves.

Carmen saw the woman move out of the corner of her eye. She lifted one of her hands off the steering wheel and swatted Joan away from the stereo.

"Leave it," she said. "Bask in the glory a little. Enjoy your voice on the radio."

Joan chuckled and sat back in her seat. Carmen was right; she should enjoy this. It was the best three minutes and twenty-five seconds of her short life. As the music dwindled into silence, Joan realized she was still grinning like a fool.

"Man, that's a killer start for Joan Devintia. And fellas... she's as hot as she sounds."

Joan rolled her eyes and muttered, "Men." She was kidding herself if she thought her album was going to sell by her talent alone. She and Jerry had already talked about it. Sex appeal was going to be important to Joan's financial success. It was always better to play up an asset than to leave it on the sidelines. Hence her future schedule of photo shoots and another music video, with less clothes, for "Girl Fight."

Not long after the song ended they arrived at Jerry's office building. Carmen checked in with Jerry while Joan got set up. No letters had come from Joan's stalker, and Jerry's assistant had called in sick – again. What was worse than the maniacal drabble of a lost mind on recipe cards? The sudden lack thereof. If he dropped off the face of the earth, he wouldn't be caught. He would get away with his crimes and give Joan the ultimate reason to look over her shoulder – possibly for the rest of her life. Carmen didn't want to live in that world.

It didn't help that Sam called her to tell her the security footage was a bust. Joan's stalker was *good*. He seemed to know the position of every camera and kept his face away from their glass lenses at all times. Even inside the private elevator – he stood very still, his nose pressed to a corner like a child in time out. The police were running background checks on all of the male staff, but it was going to take a time to process the results.

As for Carmen, it took half an hour, and Joan's singing to get her mind off everything that could go wrong. She didn't distract herself with her phone while Joan was in the live room this time. She watched the performance, and even though Joan was

184

only out to record her voice – it *was* a performance. The way Joan's mouth moved when she sang, every time she flipped her hair and took a breath was a part of the show. More than once, Carmen caught herself staring way too hard.

There was a light mood between takes. The band joked around about as much as they played. Joan was pretty confident that they already had what they needed to finish the CD, but she wouldn't be a great artist if she didn't take Jerry's creative suggestions seriously. He wanted a grittier version of the CD's last track, and when three o'clock rolled around – Jerry was satisfied with what was produced.

High fives went around the live room as Jerry called it a wrap.

Rory set his guitar down and patted Joan on the shoulder. "You gotta come over tonight. We're gonna have a little post-production party. Nothing big," he told her. "Just have a few beers and some barbeque."

Joan glanced from the Russian through the soundproof glass to Carmen. The mics were still broadcasting to the mixing booth, but the she felt like she didn't have to ask her bodyguard if they could go. It was just a small get-together with the band, what kind of harm could come from that?

"Yeah, all right."

Carmen shouldn't have been surprised by the suggestion of a party – or that Joan agreed. The celebrity lifestyle definitely was not for her, and she found herself leaning toward retiring from the bodyguard business after this again. Whatever thoughts of Joan had been running through Carmen's mind while she watched the singer stopped immediately. She couldn't consider being with Joan.

She needed calm and control, with outings in between. Not a different party every Friday, and

185

definitely not all the booze and drug use. She had her share of black-out nights, and she finally felt like she had control of those urges.

When they were done in the studio, Carmen took Joan home to change. In the penthouse, Joan's first priority were her seahorses. She checked to make sure all of them were looking as healthy as when she last left and fed them frozen krill. Unfortunately, the locks hadn't been changed yet, but it didn't look like Stan had come back. Maybe he knew Joan wasn't there... A terrifying thought.

Following the remnants of rush hour traffic, Joan and Carmen arrived at the brothers' estate. The Russian duo was born into an amount of Southern California wealth. Their two-story McMansion was complete with a Hummer, private pool, and massively ostentatious chandelier in the main hall. Joan made it as far as the unlocked front door when she was assaulted with the vestige of a surprise party.

The hall was cluttered with people dressed up for business and others dressed down for fun. Amidst flutes of champagne, beers, and other liquor; guests were chatting, smiling, and laughing.

Rory caught sight of the singer and pushed his way through a few bodies to shout. "Surprise!"

Joan grinned at the man as people applauded her. Jerry let out a whistle from across the space in celebration of his new star. This certainly wasn't what Joan had been expecting.

Joan was swarmed by some good acquaintances she had made while in San Diego. Hector and a few patrons of Dodger's were mulling about with Joan's sound crew while friends and family of the other bandmates mingled as one. Minor celebrities were in attendance, too.

Jerry introduced the singer to some of his associates: other producers, some high-profile lawyers,

186

and one very interested owner of a successful record label company. They all congratulated her on the hard work and wished her luck. It was all a little overwhelming for Joan, and if it was distressing for her – it was probably suffocating Carmen.

The amount of people and raucous raised Carmen's blood pressure and pulse. The Marine held it together on the outside, though. When she forced her mind past the overstimulation, she could admit that the guys were doing a nice thing for Joan.

Still managing to be polite Joan excused herself from the hall. Knowing Carmen was in tow, she took them into the backyard, citing a very real need for the barbeque that was promised. There was less chaos on the lantern-lighted patio since most people hadn't come for food.

Joan ate a little, still having to juggle the people who wanted to talk to her. A couple of hours since they arrived, the majority of businessmen and family were gone. They knew what was to come of a party in this neighborhood with this amount of young adults, wealth, and spare time. They were above such things. Rory and Bruce were not.

Bruce turned on their stereo system and declared the pool open before he cannonballed in – still wearing his sunglasses.

Joan had enjoyed herself up until this point, but it was a party on a Friday night. A line or two of coke was calling her name and Rory was happy to deliver. It was pretty obvious that the guitarist was already high by the time he found Joan in a lounge chair with a beer.

"Hey, honey."

Joan glanced up at him as he pulled a small bag from his pocket. Joan's nose tingled with sensation just seeing the powder. She wanted it; she didn't expect to want it so much.

Rory kneeled and poured out the contents of the pouch on the wooden armrest of her chair. It was a cool, still night. Under the few stars that could pierce the artificial light pollution of the city, the powder heaped into a mass that didn't blow away. Before he could cut it into lines, Joan sat up and leaned away from the drug.

"I'm gonna have to pass," she told him.

"Oh, come on." Dilated pupils looked disappointed in Joan. He broke out a credit card and made neat, thin lines with it. "You just finished your first CD, celebrate a little!"

Joan shook her head and got to her feet. She was still desperately tempted to taste that high, but what ecstasy could beat hearing herself on the radio that morning? What on Earth could make her happier than sharing that moment with Carmen, knowing they were growing close? Certainly not another line of empty dust.

Amped, Rory tried to salvage the lost cause. "You remember Detroit? That was a good time, wasn't it?"

Detroit was the last stop on the tour with Despite Darkness, and it certainly had been a wild night. She remembered *most* of it, but she also recalled Rory doing lines off her bare stomach.

"I'm having a good time," she countered. She didn't want to insult Rory after all the trouble he went to here, but she wasn't about to get high just to please him.

Rory didn't answer until one of the lines was snorted and gone. "Your loss, sweetheart. You know where it is if you change your mind."

Before Joan could walk away, Kevin appeared behind her. "Something wrong with your supply?"

Joan shook her head and saw that Carmen had perked up substantially. This was the first time all

188

evening that Carmen was taking an interest in anything besides nursing her bottle of water.

"I just don't feel like blow."

"You want something else? Downers maybe?" Kevin lowered his voice. "You only have to come to me, Joan." She did know. Her stash proved it. "Not that I approve, but it's my job to keep you happy, angel."

Joan narrowed her eyes just as Carmen stepped in between them. Carmen had heard more than enough. She shoved the man back and squared her shoulders as he tripped over a kiddie pool full of meltwater and beer bottles. He narrowly missed falling in.

"Still getting over that mysterious illness?" Carmen accused. The plastic bottle in her hand crinkled. "You seem a little unsteady on your feet."

Unsure of what was going on, Joan intervened. "Carmen, back off." She knew Carmen didn't like her drug use, but that didn't give the bodyguard the right to push people around.

Carmen looked down at the gentle hand on her sternum, then back to Kevin. "Sorry," she said, gruffly. Though it hurt her pride, she offered Kevin assistance and helped him to his feet. She couldn't help but wonder what Kevin looked like in a ball cap in a dark alley as she rubbed her palm on her jeans. Kevin's hand was sweaty.

The two woman had more than enough celebrating for the night and left the party together. Joan couldn't manage the energy to force Carmen to explain her bad attitude, and Carmen didn't voice her suspicions. That heavy silence went home with them, laid in their separate beds beside them, and kissed them goodnight.

CHAPTER EIGHTEEN

The next morning, Joan got the call that the locks were changed. Instead of sharing a quiet breakfast with Carmen, she spent the morning hours on the phone with her parents. They told her all about seeing their little girl's name in lights and being so proud of her. They asked when they could fly up to see her, but Joan resurrected an old habit of lying. She wasn't going to be in San Diego tomorrow, she told them, or for the rest of the week that matter... But she promised they would catch up soon. She had to lie to keep them and her secrets safe.

In reality, Jerry gave her and the band the week off. As soon as the CD was ready to drop, Joan would be too busy for house calls. Jerry was scheduling interviews, finalizing tour details, and auditioning replacement drummers that would also have to get past Joan. If nothing else, she was sure that she would see her family when she was in southeast leg of her tour.

After Joan got her things packed, Carmen took her to the Marmax building. They stopped at the security desk to swap out keys and cards. The officer informed them that maintenance added a jimmy-proof deadbolt to the door. As soon as they were up there, Carmen inspected the installations.

Joan watched her bodyguard lock the new deadbolt, pull and push on the door with force, then unlock the bolt again. Carmen checked each locking mechanism individually, three times, in the same order. Joan cocked her head and tried to dim her smile.

"I don't think the zombies are getting in," she teased.

Carmen laughed once and pulled herself away from her compulsion. "Zombies are not in my contract."

"I'll get Jerry on that."

Carmen folded her arms and shifted on her feet. "I know you don't have to go to the studio this week, but if there's anything you want to do, just fill me in."

Joan knew the drill, but it was nice to see that Carmen was still just as adamant about performing her job as she had been on the very first day. She was glad to be home, but Carmen's apartment was a pleasant change of pace. It wasn't as foreign and generic as a hotel room, but it also wasn't toxic like her bandmate's mansion would have been. Had she shown her appreciation enough?

"Thank you for letting me stay with you," Joan said, closing some distance so they could talk.

Carmen nodded. "Of course. I hope my little hole in the wall was better than a hotel room."

"It was great," Joan responded. She leaned in toward Carmen and gently wrapped her arms around the other woman, resting her hands across Carmen's broad shoulders.

Carmen stiffened up the smallest amount before relaxing. After a moment, she pulled her arms up around Joan to return the hug. Not just anyone could get so close to Carmen without her freezing.

Joan pursed her lips when she realized that she taxed Carmen into an action that was uncomfortable for her. It was just like when she had taken Carmen's hand; there was hesitation before surrender. Maybe Carmen would relax more around her in time. Joan rubbed one thumb between the woman's shoulder blades before she pulled back.

"Sorry," she whispered.

"It's all right." Carmen simply wasn't used to physical contact because she had avoided it for so long.

Joan offered Carmen free range of the place for a few hours if she wanted. The two relaxed for an afternoon before Carmen went her own way. Joan didn't have many plans for the week. Tomorrow, she'd go running with Carmen. Monday, she would try to get Carmen to shop with her.

Of course, Carmen would go simply because that's what Joan had to do for the day. But Joan wanted more from Carmen than that…. She wanted to know what Carmen thought about *this* outfit, or *that* one. She wanted to see it in Carmen's face when she came around the dressing room door in a black cocktail dress, or hear it in her laughter when Joan left that same room in mom jeans and wearing the world's largest sun hat. She wanted to stop in that chocolate boutique she never found the time to try and debate not-so-seriously between chocolate-covered bacon and chocolate-covered potato chips, just to choose a caramel apple, have it cut into slices, and share it. She wanted to listen to Carmen whine about having to help carry bags of clothes up 12 *whole* flights of stairs and affectionately point out that they had taken the elevator.

Like most celebrities, Joan got everything she wanted, which was a problem. Because on Tuesday, Joan decided she wanted Monday again. Not the dressing room antics, or the dessert, just the good company. Carmen made her wonder why she hadn't written any positive songs about love.

Tuesday afternoon, miles away, Carmen barely finished cutting a sandwich in half when her phone started buzzing. It shouldn't have been Joan calling her, because the woman had been all about an in-home spa afternoon to relax. When the name came up on the screen, she immediately swiped to answer.

"I thought we were past the days of you interrupting my meals," she joked.

Sam laughed. "I don't think we'll ever be past those days."

"So, what's up?"

"Sit rep. I need you to come down to the station as soon as you can," he explained.

"Sounds serious."

"It is. We managed to pull a partial print off the note in Joan's penthouse, and it flagged some hits. Since you said you might have seen him in Los Angeles, I put together some profiles for you to look at."

Carmen's ears began to warm as her throat went dry. If Sam had pictures and profiles, it was up to her to identify the stalker. She hadn't gotten a good look at the guy's face in Los Angeles – he was too busy running from her for that. What if it wasn't enough?

"Yeah, okay. I'll be there soon," she agreed after a moment.

"Good. I'll see you then."

Carmen set her phone back on the counter and tore off a section of wax paper to wrap up her food. With lunch hour traffic to contend with, she was going to have to eat on the run. Investigating leads made her want to check on Joan, so she sent the woman a text while she was still parked. When Joan texted her back, Carmen broke the law to check it while she drove. She read the message at a stop light and took a deep breath when she learned that Joan was fine.

The San Diego traffic gods deemed her sacrifice worthy and didn't throw too much traffic in

Carmen's way. Before long, she walked into the police station and asked for Sam at the front desk.

She sat for a few minutes until he came out, and then they went back to his desk together. Despite the same training and scrutiny, Sam still wasn't one for spitting and polishing his work space. He was in the grips of stockpiling papers, folders, yellow highlighters – and the obsession was winning.

"Thanks for coming down here so quick," Sam said as they sat down. "It's best if we can get Joan's stalker identified sooner, rather than later."

"Yeah, I'll take a look and see if any of them look familiar." Eyes narrowed at the mess, Carmen picked up a stack of forms and moved them out of her line of sight.

Sam grabbed one of the files on his desk and thumbed through it before producing a couple sheets of paper. He reached over and laid the papers in front of Carmen, facing her. Each one had six pictures of white men on it.

Carmen looked over each photo carefully, racking her brain for specific details about the man she'd seen so she could match him to one of those sitting before her. She had hoped to see Kevin Lewis' face staring back at her. The man was just close enough to Joan, had the right connections… but his picture wasn't in the dozen she was looking at.

"Sam, I don't recognize any of these guys." Carmen sat back and folded her arms over her chest. "Why isn't Kevin Lewis here? Did you check him out?"

"Yeah, we did. Nothing came back on him, though. It's not him, Carmen."

Carmen huffed before she continued to look at the pictures. She willed one of them to stand out. If she wasn't able to identify him, that put Joan at risk longer. She'd seen him, damn it, and it should have

194

been easy to spot him because of that. However, her first gut instinct on the stalker's identity had been completely wrong. What if she was wrong again and it got Joan hurt – or worse?

There was so much going on in the station already: people talking, walking around, phones ringing. That added to the heavy weight of being the only one who had a chance of identifying the stalker. It was getting hard for Carmen to concentrate.

"Carmen?" Sam prodded gently, sensing a rising level of distress in his friend.

"Sam, I… I can't," she shook her head. "I can't."

"It's okay," Sam tried to reassure her. "If none of these guys look familiar, then they just don't look familiar."

"It's not okay, though," Carmen fired back, banging her fist on the desk and rattling a cup of pencils. "I can't identify this guy, so you can't go arrest him. That leaves Joan in danger. She's relying on me to keep her safe."

"There's only so much that you can do. If you didn't get a good enough look at him in Los Angeles, then there's no way you're going to be able to identify him. We'll keep our feet on the ground and keep looking for him."

"And if that's not good enough?"

"It's going to have to be."

Carmen nodded, though she didn't really accept that as the final answer. She couldn't help but think of the worst as she left the police station. If only she'd managed to get a better look at the man that ran from her in Los Angeles, they could be putting this case to rest.

~*~

195

That night, Joan stood at her balcony with her hands resting on the cold railing. Aside from the fact that she was on a break, things seemed more quiet than normal. Stalker Stan hadn't done a thing since being inside her apartment days ago. Maybe he got a clue, or a semi-normal brain, or a new obsession. The latter was far more likely.

She knew she would have a lot less to worry about if he was gone for good, but one thing about his absence pained her. Carmen. Without him, Jerry wouldn't need to keep her employed like this. Joan would miss the other woman; she missed her now.

Joan fished her phone from her jean pocket and brought up Carmen's contact information. After half a minute of staring, she let the device go dark and looked out at the cityscape. Colored, artificial light rose high above the sounds of cars and boat horns from the coast. Joan set her phone on the ledge and tapped her fingers on the device. The light coming from her penthouse illuminated a pattern of smudges on the black screen. Carmen's phone would have been spotless.

Huffing at herself, she wiped her phone on her designer shirt until it was clean. Joan was over her indecisiveness, so she typed out a message and hit send.

i need you tonight

She couldn't say much more than that. She dismissed the opportunity to lie, knowing that she could have made something up that had to do with Stan. That would have gotten Carmen over here fast enough, but she wanted to make her intentions clear to the other woman. But as soon as she reread the text, she frowned at her informality. She shouldn't have turned off auto-capitalize, and she forgot a period.

196

Across the city, Carmen typed a complete sentence.

On my way.

Seeing the text message from Joan, Carmen had automatically assumed that something was wrong. Of course something had to be wrong – why else would Joan need her?

Carmen grabbed her things and pocketed them before heading out of the apartment. Her Matrix movie marathon was long forgotten. She half-jumped, half-jogged down the flight of stairs and got to her SUV. The elevator ride was the longest part of the trip by far.

Joan fell under the rule of the digital clock on her phone as she paced her apartment, waiting for the pixelated minutes to go by. Maybe she was rushing this. Maybe time was going way too slow. Joan's head shot up at a sudden knock. She smiled as Carmen let herself into the penthouse.

"Hey," Carmen greeted. She scanned the area, looking for danger in any form it took. There was no one else around and nothing white or powdery on any flat surface. "Everything okay?"

Joan furrowed her eyebrows before she realized how her text must have come off. "Oh. Yeah," she answered, stepping toward the other woman. "I... just..." Wanted to fuck everything up. Joan struggled to find the right words inside the stuffy penthouse. The situation had seemed so much clearer while she had been standing on the balcony. "Can we go outside?"

Carmen surveyed Joan as if she were trying to determine if Joan was a noncombatant or not. Who knew what was hiding under that heathered gray baseball tee? Who knew how strong Joan's necklace when the chain was wrapped around someone else's neck? "Yeah, sure," Carmen answered. She didn't know why she was on edge as she pulled open the sliding glass door for them. There was no battlefield here, no fight. What was behind that seemingly urgent text?

Joan tried and failed to get a grip on herself. She would have sold her favorite guitar for an ounce of the confidence she had in the middle of a stage in front of thousands of people. If Carmen didn't have such an issue with touch, Joan might have just showed the other woman what she couldn't verbalize. Both expressions of affection involved her lips.

Perhaps if she started out slow on both accounts... Tip of the spear, as Carmen would say.

Joan approached Carmen and reached out for the other woman's hand as she spoke quietly, tentatively. "I've been thinking about that list-" She paused when she felt Carmen's fingertips press into her skin, returning the embrace. "I think I know a way to shorten it, *significantly*." Joan smiled coyly. She had watched her seahorses do this dance too many times to forget the next step.

In one, easy movement, she repositioned their hands so that their fingers were intertwined and leaned into Carmen's very personal space. "I think... girlfriend covers about all of it." Their noses touched before Joan closed her eyes.

Earth moved, fire raced when their lips connected like a shifting fault line. For once, Carmen was the taller of the two. Combat boots had the advantage over socks this time. Carmen reached out for the balcony to steady herself. This wasn't any kiss. This was a rockslide, an earthquake. It was a volcano named Joan – and Carmen held onto the ledge like she was going to be swept away.

Short nails scratching over the metal rail, Carmen wanted and feared the kiss continuing. Red flags were being thrown up by her overactive mind. She let go of Joan's hand and stepped back.

"Joan... I- I can't do this. I can't keep up with the parties every week, and I won't watch you destroy yourself with drugs." Carmen had walked too close to the fiery edge and wrote her apology in ash with words a Marine shouldn't say. "Can't" wasn't supposed to be in her dictionary.

The pale hand reaching for Carmen's waist was left in the open air as Joan struggled to comprehend why Carmen was slowly backing away. It was true, they didn't line up nicely and neatly on every point, but there were good for each other. Weren't they?

"Carmen?" Joan felt a bit like she was trying to comfort a cornered animal. "Give me a chance," she begged. She wouldn't give chase beyond the confines of her balcony if Carmen was really serious, but she had to try. She had to fight for the woman she cared about.

"I'm sorry, Joan." Carmen had stepped onto the field totally unprepared for this. She had expected a problem she could fix. Maybe some unnamed danger from Joan's stalker that she could intercept or an inclination for Joan's bad habits that she could help to curb. She felt awful, mostly because she felt like striding forward and reconnecting their lips. Instead, she turned to leave.

Joan stood tall as she watched Carmen walk away. Faced with the painful facts, she thought about what Carmen said. She had no plans to cut back on partying or drugs; she had just been laying low while Stalker Stan had it out for her. Now it didn't seem to matter that she would have tried to give it up if that was what Carmen wanted. For dog tags and skull boxers... she would have tried.

So wrapped up in thinking how things had gone so wrong, Joan suddenly came around to the present and ran to the other edge of the balcony. She stared down, hunting the entrance to the parking garage. For ten o'clock on a Tuesday night there was a fair amount of people, coming and going, outside the Marmax building. Maybe Carmen hadn't left yet. Maybe Carmen changed her mind somewhere around the seventh floor, and she was on the ride back up.

The answer came a few seconds later as Carmen's SUV pulled out of the garage and drove onto the street. Joan's heart sank as she watched, with tears in her eyes, a soldier's steadfast retreat.

Carmen shook her head as she left the Marmax building in rearview mirror. She'd been presented with an opportunity – honestly one of the best opportunities that had been offered to her – and threw it away like nothing. She had her reasons, she tried to remind herself. Digging her nails into the leather of her steering wheel, she grit her teeth. She had her reasons.

Turning the wheel right, she had to slam on the breaks to stop from hitting some asshole pedestrian that was crossing the street at the wrong time. She hit her fist on the horn and barely felt her hand connect despite the bruising force.

"Hey, get out of the way!"

The man looked up and kept walking calmly at the same pace. Carmen cursed to herself in a mixture of Spanish and English, which only stopped when she was finally able to turn.

When Joan lost sight of Carmen's tail lights, she didn't really know what to do with herself. That childish, vindictive side of herself told her to get high. Drugs would chase away the pain for a while, but they were clearly also part of the problem.

"Fuck it," she muttered and walked back into

200

her apartment. She pulled off her clothes and dressed into skinny jeans just so they could be tucked into her favorite knee high boots. After tugging on a leather jacket over a black camisole, she checked herself out in her full-length mirror. Her lipstick was smudged from kissing Carmen. With one swipe of her thumb, she fixed the mess. She touched up her lips and avoided looking herself in the eyes as much as she could.

She was going out. Her favorite Thai dinner was calling her name, and she sure-as-fuck wasn't going to ask Carmen to escort her. Some fresh air would clear her head, and sometime between ordering and getting the check – she hoped to get some semblance of her life without Carmen and Stan back. Fate knew one of them would probably be gone from her life very soon.

Joan got to the corner of the Marmax building and waited to hail a taxi. A yellow mini-coup had just rounded the corner when she found herself on the sidewalk with an all-female group of bar-hoppers.

"No, I'm telling you, I know her."

Joan listened as one of the woman whispered to her companions.

"That's Joan Devintia..."

She smiled to herself before one of the group found the courage to approach. Amidst brief small talk, Joan hailed the slow-moving taxi and let the women have it. They seemed a little upset to be taking the ride from her, but she told them she would get the next one. In better spirits after interacting with some pleasant fans, Joan decided she would make some of the trip on foot. It was too nice of an evening to spend it watching a growing meter.

As much as she wanted Carmen, she had made promises to herself that she couldn't break. Giving up music and the life that came with it was out of the question. There would always be parties she was invited to and drugs at those parties she'd be tempted to do. With luck, there would always be concerts and fans. Some of which would approach her on the street like those friendly women had just done. She'd made herself too recognizable, rocking a stark undercut and a leather jacket.

It wouldn't be fair to ask Carmen to constantly put herself in situations that made her uncomfortable. Carmen had been through so much and done so much for Joan already.

~*~

Get it together, Savedra. You're acting ridiculous.
What on Earth was she doing? Carmen was sitting in her parked SUV, exhaust rolling upwards into the darkness as she idled in her apartment parking lot. A certain penthouse was shouting her name to come back. Carmen desperately wanted to answer the call. But she had to stick to her guns. Right?

She couldn't date a rock star. There were too many parties and being around while Joan got high, once a week or more, had zero appeal. Drugs broke people down, killed them. She couldn't go shopping with Joan and watch her buy a new jacket with the same credit card she cut coke with.

But hadn't Joan asked for a chance? That meant she may have been willing to give it up, or at least try to. That had to count for something.

Carmen couldn't ask her to do that, though. A rock star's life was pretty universal, and that was just as true for Joan as anyone else. The only thing she could rightly push for was a drug-free life, and Joan should have done that anyway, simply for her health.

God damn it. You're full of shit and you know it. Quit hiding behind excuses, that's not who you are.
It wasn't the partying that kept her from Joan.

No, Carmen was scared. The last person she'd been close with abandoned her when she needed help the most, and it had been devastating.

She and Cheyenne had been together since her first deployment. The two had been off and on through high school with other relationships in between, but got more serious during and after the Marine's time at boot camp. Though she had told Cheyenne she didn't expect the other woman to wait while she was overseas, Cheyenne had insisted on it. They had been rowdy and wild in their time together, and it was assumed that would never change.

When given leave to return Stateside for a couple of weeks, Carmen spent that time with Cheyenne. They indulged in whatever would be fun, because they had to pack months' worth of time into just a couple of short weeks. Her first few trips home were great. The only thing out of the ordinary was the fact that Carmen spent several months away at a time.

Then, after seeing live combat and going through extreme stress missions, Carmen's reservations took ahold of her. She wasn't as willing to go out to the bar every night while she was Stateside. All she wanted was to stay somewhere quiet, away from people. Cheyenne partially adjusted, but did so with protest. What she wanted was their fast and furious lifestyle, not to sit home with nothing to do.

The shallow relationship ended on the day that Carmen realized tragedy sold more roses than romantic love.

At the Stateside memorial service for her squad mates, Cheyenne called it quits. She walked away from Carmen, who was still bandaged and stone-faced, as they were about to go into the church – where God and country were waiting. Sam's wife pushed the Staff Sergeant's wheelchair in just before them, and trying to be close like Sam and Maria were,

Cheyenne reached for Carmen's free hand when the Marine wasn't looking. Carmen's voice got a little too loud in front of a few too many people when she told Cheyenne not to touch her. That was the last of many offences that began after overseas deployment. Cheyenne couldn't handle the panicky, angry side of Carmen for another second. The long road to being healthy wasn't one Cheyenne wanted to walk down.

Since there was no quick fix to panic attacks, no Band-Aids for depression, no reset button on life, Carmen was left to stare at the patriotic wreathes and roses sitting against the base of a sign that listed the day's services. Her friends, her brothers were on that list, and it wasn't until Maria came back out to get her that she believed she could take another step forward.

But Joan wasn't Cheyenne. Joan was patient and understanding. When she reached out for Carmen, she did so slowly and waited for Carmen to relax before cementing the physical contact. Joan spit fire, and played loud. Her public life was everything Carmen should have stayed away from, but when it was just the two of them – it was *just* the two of them. When she sang, there were no jarring sounds that could pierce Joan's voice. Joan's perfume was incomparable to the smell of gunpowder or blood. Above all else, nothing made Carmen stare and zone out quite like Joan's smile.

"*Mujer de puta*," she swore at herself.

With a quick gear change, she drove out of her parking spot. Of course she had to go back. How could she not?

Head clear again, she focused on the road. She didn't know what she would say when she got there, but her heart thrummed with a giddy sensation. Halfway between a deep breath and a nervous laugh, her stomach dropped as a thought stormed to the front of her mind. That man she yelled at while he was crossing the road... He wasn't wearing a red tie, but he was familiar.

She knew exactly who he was.

"Oh, shit!" she cursed again, pressing the gas pedal further down.

CHAPTER NINETEEN

"Hello, Joan."

Joan whipped around, terror shooting through her at the sound of Stan's voice. She locked eyes with her stalker, took a step back, and felt like she was falling. Her heel slipped off the curb, causing her to tumble into the street. Cold cement bit the underside of her hands as she pushed herself back up.

"Leave me alone," she threatened, voice wavering. God, what she wouldn't have given to be with Carmen right now. Righteous indignation trickled into her cocktail of fear and pain. She was not invincible. What had brought her out here anyway, some hurt pride?

"Leave you alone?" Stan questioned her with childlike confusion. "I can't do that, my angel." He jumped off the curb, landing with the sharp crack of leather dress shoes that were too big for his feet.

Surveying the road, Joan targeted the far sidewalk. If she ran, she was afraid that it would escalate the encounter into a race she couldn't win. A car was on the approach, taking the city street at fast but legal speeds. She could use the vehicle as a barrier, if she timed it right. She walked at a brisk pace, and Stan followed – talking the entire time.

"You and I are meant to be together. Don't you see? We share something special, something other people can't even begin to comprehend. I didn't understand it myself, at first. But whenever the pain comes crawling in- crawling…" Stan paused, a finger coming to his temple and digging in like he could unscramble his thoughts if he pushed hard enough.

Joan grabbed the phone from her pocket. She wasn't steady enough to scroll through over a hundred contacts. Instead, she used the speech recognition program and spoke at the chime.

"Call Carmen." That seemed to be all Stan needed to snap out of his trance. A horn blared as the car swerved to avoid him. Her command to failed. She was about to try again, but the iPhone was smacked from her hands. It clattered to the ground, and Joan cringed as Stan pierced the screen with his heel. Glass, plastic, and hope scattered in jagged pieces.

Stan smiled. "It's your voice, Joan! Your voice calls me back, every time."

"Get away from me!" she screamed, giving him that voice he loved in such a bitter way. She leapt to the sidewalk and broke into a jog, searching for an escape. Just as she feared, running only made him more excited.

"Ready?" he husked. "*Set*. Start." It was then that Joan realized he was quoting her own lyrics at her. "Cut to the chase. My favorite part!"

Joan listened to his laughter as she ran to the nearest building. It was a post office, and it was closed. The doors were probably locked, so she didn't even try them. Every building in the strip mall was dark, but lights were just beyond the next intersection. If she could just make it to the fast food joint on the corner, she could get help.

Unfortunately, she never made it that far. With his longer strides, Stan got a grip on Joan that she was familiar with. His fingers locked around her bicep as he jerked her to a stop. Her mind reeled and fell into an old world of apologizing to her abuser.

"I'm sorry. I'm sorry." She trembled as her eyes watered.

"You're sorry? You ignore me, hire a bodyguard, yell at me… and you want me to forgive you?"

Joan nodded, causing a tear to roll down her cheek. Disgust sat in her stomach, kicking and punching its way through her self-confidence. Her arm began to ache, and instead of giving into the whimper behind her lips – it reminded her of the power in pain.

She didn't go to the restaurant in her home town with a black eye for nothing. She didn't work ten hours a day to let a thousand negative feelings hold her back from her dreams. She didn't shave her head every two weeks to forget how fucking strong she was now.

Joan was done playing Stan's game, even if he wasn't.

"All right, Joan. I forgive you."

"Good," she whispered. The grip on her arm loosened, but he was still holding on. "You know me pretty well, don't you? You know I like Thai. I'm headed to The Orchid right now. I'm sorry I haven't invited you out before, but why don't you come with me?" She squeezed her left hand into a fist at the apology, but the act was necessary. Being nice to her ex, being remorseful, ended his fits sooner. All Joan had to do was keep Stan docile enough to get help.

Stan narrowed his exhausted-looking eyes as a trio of cars passed them. "It would be wonderful to sit at the same booth this time." His words made Joan shiver. This time. How many times had Stan been around without Joan knowing it?

"Why don't we keep walking?" she suggested. Wiping away her tears and hoping her makeup hadn't run too badly, she vowed that she wouldn't cry again no matter how the night turned out.

Stan steered them across the street and got them back on the correct sidewalk. If they made it all the way to The Orchid, Joan could probably get a message to the wait staff. In the meantime, she scoured the area for someone who could help. She got distracted by a collection of dark stains on Stan's sweatshirt, marking him as a messy eater. At least she hoped the spots were from food and not blood.

Every time headlights approached, Joan felt a tingle go up her spine. None of the vehicles slowed unless they were turning or stopping at a light. She racked her mind for something that would spark a rational conversation, but she didn't want to talk Stan. She didn't even want to learn his name.

"So…" Joan squeezed her eyes shut tight as she made her mouth form the words. "You're a big fan, huh?"

"Oh, the biggest." In tune, Stan hummed some of her music to her. If he noticed Joan's grimace, it didn't bother him. "I know all of your songs by heart. At least, the ones I've heard. There are still two tracks on *Snowball Earth* that I haven't been able to listen to yet."

Feeling exposed by Stan's knowledge of her music, Joan paled. How had he managed to get his hands on all of those songs? Did Stan work in the studio? Did it matter anymore?

"Like it so far?" Joan asked. This was one critic she didn't want to disappoint.

"It's magnificent!" Stan secured his grip on Joan, bringing his free hand to the arm he had trapped. "You're going to be huge, Joan. People everywhere are going to love you, but – don't forget – I loved you *first*."

Joan swallowed. She could barely push past the lump in her throat to keep him talking, but she knew she had to.

"I won't forget."

"Ever since that first concert... Atlanta. Despite Darkness sold out... Over twenty thousand people, and I was one of them. Oh, but I'm sure I stood out to you, didn't I?"

Joan nodded stiffly. "You always do." At the club, in The Orchid, on the street – Stan stood out like a lighthouse above the body crush of ever-pressing waves. She was drowning again.

"Change of plans, my angel."

Without any more warning, Stan drove the singer into an alley of patched up brickwork and trash bags full to bursting. At the sight of an older, burgundy sedan, Joan got loud. She knew in her heart that it was Stan's junker, and if he got her into it, she was dead.

"What are you doing? Stop it! Let me go!"

"We're not going to The Orchid," he snarled. As if that weren't obvious. "I want you to sing for me. Alone."

Dragging Joan to the car, he opened a back door. Sitting on the threadbare upholstery was a roll of silver duct tape. While the woman struggled, he pulled a strip free with his teeth. The second he stood tall again, Joan punched him in the jaw.

She had never raised a hand to David, but she had grown since then. With the same fury she used in her music, she pulled back to strike again. He left the roll of duct tape hanging from bloodied teeth as he caught her fist.

Stan spun her around and shoved her onto the trunk of his car. Her chin hit the metal and shot lights into her skull. Dazed, Joan listened to the man tear a piece of tape, and then another, and another. By the time she came around, her wrists were secured behind her.

"Fuck you!" she screamed. As Stan threw her into his car, she was one-part banshee and ninety-nine-

210

parts pissed off. "You'll never fucking have me, you sick fuck!" He slammed the door on her. "I would rather cut my own tongue out than sing for you!"

Stan slid into the driver's seat and responded to the muffled yelling he heard. "Singing or screaming, it's still your voice, Joan. It's always your voice."

Joan clamped her jaw shut. She looked down to where the door handle should have been. The area was cut up and scrapped silver again with metal tools. She saw that the mechanism had been removed and began pushing herself across the backseat until she collided with the other door. As she tried to get her hands into position, she yelped when the car peeled out of the alley.

Frantic and panting, she looked over her shoulder as she tried to feel for the door handle. The moment something sharp punctured her forearm, she knew that the door was just as tampered with as the last. So, she tried to free herself from the restraints.

The thick tape pinched and dug into her, but she couldn't stop. She worked her hands back and forth, up and down, twisting them and pulling while Stan drove through the city. Passing street lights shone in the sweat on her face. More often than not, when the orange light illuminated the interior of the car, she caught Stan's eyes staring at her through the rearview mirror.

The minutes ate away at Joan. They could be the last of her life, and there was so much she hadn't done. She wasn't ready to die, so when Stan slowed the car and pulled into a closed down motel, she got ready to shove a three-inch heel into the soft tissue of his stomach. But Stan was wise to her. When he got out of the car, he went to the door she was leaning on. She couldn't move in time and he grabbed her.

Joan wasn't sure how long they had been driving, but she recognized the outskirts of San Diego.

She screamed at the familiar skyline as Stan forced her toward his screwed up idea of a one-on-one show.

~*~

As soon as Carmen got back to the Marmax building, she jumped out of the SUV and bolted past the front desk. If she could have run up to the twelfth floor faster than the elevator could travel, she would have taken the stairs. Instead, she paced inside the steel box and pushed herself out the doors when there was a space wide enough.

She sprinted to the penthouse, not bothering to announce her presence before letting herself in. "Joan!" she called as she pushed the door open. "Joan!" Carmen scoured the apartment, but no one was there.

Fuming, she pulled out her phone. Trying to call Joan again would just be a waste of time, so she called Sam.

After the first ring, the line picked up. "Hey, Carmen, I was-"

"Sam!" she interrupted. "He has Joan!" Carmen went back out of the penthouse and started toward the elevator again.

"What? Who has her?" he questioned.

"The stalker! I left after we had a little... disagreement." That detail wasn't important, but Carmen couldn't help telling Sam of her distress as she waited outside the elevator. "We were both upset. Then I realized I passed him – he was walking toward the Marmax building. Joan's not in her penthouse, and you *know* he managed to get in before." Carmen hoped Sam was keeping up with all of this.

"Maybe she went for a walk or to get some food."

Carmen grunted, frustration gripping at her

chest. "Sam! Trust me on this, I know he has her."

"Okay, okay. Calm down a little. I was going to call you because we got some more information." He paused to take a breath, but Carmen was holding hers. "We finally heard back from New York, best print match out of the whole group. We did some cross-referencing, and we got a local address."

"Give me the address," she demanded, pushing the button to open the elevator doors.

"Carmen, you need to leave it to us."

"Sam! The address!"

There was silence on the other end for long moments before he spoke again. "All right, but don't do anything unreasonable."

After getting what she needed, she hung up on her friend and stepped inside the elevator. On the long ride down, she wondered if she had locked Joan's apartment again. She wasn't sure she had.

CHAPTER TWENTY

Joan didn't make it easy on her captor. She fought without fear of him striking back. As he tried to wrangle her towards one of the abandoned motel rooms, she was a mix of dead weight and bad temperament.

"I'm gonna take one of those precious goddamn ties you love so much and choke you with it! I'll take the first copy of *Snowball Earth* I get, break it, and cut off your fucking dick with the pieces!"

Stan laughed at her ferocity. He manhandled her into the middle suite where Joan's fire-storm attitude dwindled. Everywhere she looked she saw herself. On the walls. On the floor. On the lumpy spring mattress. The photographs varied in quality and size. Some had been printed on expensive gloss paper, while others had the shoddy look of an ink printer about to run out of yellow. Several pictures were defaced, quite literally, with unexplained tears and neat cuts through her smiling features.

Joan was going to die fulfilling a psychopath's only wish.

When she heard the door lock slam into position behind her, she jumped. Stan had a wicked grin on his face, and they both quieted. He walked to Joan and shoved her into a sitting position on the bed. With one hand pressed to her shoulder to keep her down, he tilted his chin and looked around. The shrine to her was glorious, and now she could finally see it, too.

"What do you think, my angel?" he asked. "Isn't it magnificent?"

The bitter taste in the back of Joan's mouth reminded her a lot of coke. But there was no white, powdered immortality on its way to numb her taste buds. Reality was hard to swallow.

"It's... It's..." Her eyes welled with tears. In an instant, Stan was as comforting as a psychopath could be.

"Don't cry, my angel. You should be happy." He kneeled in front of his obsession and placed a hand on her cheek. "We're together now."

"Fuck you," Joan spat. She had promised herself she wasn't going to cry, so she bucked up. Turning out of Stan's hand, she looked around the room for a scrap of hope. On a desk, she found a section of a menu from The Orchid instead. Her usual orders were circled in bold, black ink. She was so fucked.

Scorned, he took another quick turn. "There was something you never answered me." He reached inside his jacket and Joan leaned back. She watched a vein in Stan's hand twitch as he tightened his grip around something. "Do angels bleed?"

Finally revealed, Joan came face to face with a Bowie knife that would make any collector proud. Every artist had to pick the right tool for their craft. For Joan, she loved her custom, Bone White Les Paul; mahogany body, maple top, with all the chrome hardware she could want. In Stan's case, he was going to carve his art with a fixed, stainless steel blade. The handle was decorated with the unmistakable gleam of mother-of-pearl, making both instruments white.

Joan renewed her struggle against the tape, but her arms were exhausted. She went at the restraints like she was about to play the most painful, finger-bloodying riff she could imagine. She would just have to power through it. No matter what Stan did to her, she couldn't stop fighting.

"Be still, now," Stan growled.

She only managed to get to her feet for a second, before her ass hit the mattress again. He was strong and driven to go through with his fantasy. Joan leaned back again and spit in his face.

"Go *fuck* yourself!"

He wiped his cheek before placing the knife against Joan's collarbone. "You're going to regret that." His temper was out of control as he broke Joan's skin with the tip of the blade, pushing it as far as an inch before Joan fell back onto the bed to get away.

Angels did bleed. They felt pain, too.

Joan gasped as the red liquid that had sparked Stan's curiosity trickled to her shirt. Adrenaline moved to circumvent the sudden, piercing hurt, but she couldn't have much left.

"Fuck you!" she repeated, unaware that new tears were flowing freely now.

Stan chuckled. "God, you're so pretty when you're mad." He wasn't fazed in the least as he tried to get control of Joan. She was moving too much for him to make the practiced cuts that he wanted to.

Just as he got a grip around her throat, both of them heard banging. It was far away, at first, but when it moved closer – Joan heard her name being shouted like she was the only thing on Carmen's list.

"Carmen!" Joan cried back. "Carm-" The hand around her throat constricted, choking the voice Stan loved so much.

"No, no," he began to whine. "You're mine. That pretty voice is for me."

Carmen's yelling got louder as she narrowed in on the correct door. "Joan!"

Stan and Joan heard Carmen attack the door of the room next to theirs. With stage lights beginning to flash behind her eyes, Joan imagined Carmen

216

kicking all the doors open to get to her. Reeling from the trauma of the night, it was a nice thought to die with. Carmen had come to save her.

When their door slammed open, Stan loosened up on Joan. Carmen aimed her gun right for the man that was not Kevin as she listened to Joan cough.

"Back off!" she demanded. Carmen had been so sure that Kevin was the perpetrator that she couldn't fire without buying herself the time to think it through.

The stranger turned away from his prize and got to his feet. "Get out of here! You can't be here!"

Carmen took a step forward. "Drop the fucking knife!"

"I won't!" he roared, on the verge of a psychotic tantrum. "I won't let you take her from me! She's mine!"

"Put the motherfucking knife down!" She flipped the safety off and drew closer. Nightmares waited at the end of her barrel. Carmen never took a life without suffering the effects, but if she didn't act, her nightmares would be about Joan screaming for her.

The situation was primed and volatile, but Carmen's focus was shaken. She looked away from the stalker's center mass and watched Joan gasp for breath. Blonde hair stuck to the woman's lips as she mouthed Camren's name. The Marine wasn't close enough to hear it spoken, but the stalker was.

He turned on Joan, brandishing the knife high above his head. One way or another, he was going to have his way.

The ear-splitting crack of a round broke Stan's concentration. He froze, surprise plain on his face. Blood dripped from a bullet wound in his right side. Seconds ticked by, before he became enraged again.

He went to finish plunging the knife into Joan. Another shot went off, this one hitting him at chest level.

It was the second hit that did the most damage. The knife rolled out of his hand and dropped to the floor. He staggered a couple of steps to the side, wheezing for air that his punctured lung couldn't hold. His legs went out from under him, and he collapsed.

While the man attempted and failed to pull himself up, getting weaker each time, Carmen lowered her weapon. She turned the safety back on and went to Joan.

The rocker was upright before Carmen got there, her eyes fixed on the man dying on the ugly, outdated carpet. Angels bled, and he was definitely doing that. Did that make him…

"I'm so sorry, Joan." Carmen's apology pulled Joan away from the carnage.

"Sorry?" Joan rasped. "Sorry for what?"

Carmen looked too scared to answer as she threw off her coat and reached for the hem of her t-shirt. Joan turned her head away, in so much shock that she couldn't figure out why Carmen was undressing.

When she felt soft material pressed to the cut on her collarbone, she glanced back to find Carmen trying to staunch her bleeding with a shirt and still wearing a tank top. Joan almost laughed. Instead, she complained.

"My hands."

Carmen was so distracted by the injury that she hadn't realized Joan was tied up. She let the shirt fall as she tucked her gun into her waistband. She climbed onto the bed and used her keys to tear the duct tape apart, knowing better than to get the attempted murder weapon for that. With care, she scarcely took a breath and pulled the tape free of Joan's bruised wrists.

She went back to applying pressure to Joan's cut, and then whispered, "Hold this." When Joan complied, Carmen laid a hand under Joan's chin to get a good look at the singer. She moved the woman's face from side to side. She eyed every visible inch of Joan, knowing her time was short. Help was coming.

Gently, she reached up, moving Joan's hair away from the corner of her mouth. Her thumb stayed in place on the woman's jaw. Before she could think of something to say or get the courage to make a move against those beautiful lips, Joan used them to speak.

"How did you know?"

"I saw him on my way home, but I didn't realize it. I- I was too upset." Carmen shook her head at her foolishness. "I've seen him before, when we were in L.A." Her explanation faltered when she heard sirens approaching. Swallowing, she dropped her hand to the woman's shoulder. Joan was quivering under her fingers.

"Joan, listen to me. When the police get here, they're going to put me in handcuffs-"

"What?" Shocked, Joan shook her head. Mentally exhausted and physically unwell, she couldn't tolerate more stress. "Why would they arrest you?"

"I just *killed* someone, Joan. If you discharge a gun and hit someone, you go to jail whether it's in defense of someone or not. I'll probably be there overnight, less time if Sam can pull some strings for me." The wailing sirens were so close. Carmen knew their time was up. She wiped the tears off of Joan's chin before getting to her feet and backing away.

Doors slammed, people shouted outside.

Carmen tried to smile. "You'll have to go to the station to give a statement, but you'll get good medical attention first. Call Jerry, all right?" Joan looked dazed. "Hey… everything is going to be okay."

As the door opened and Carmen raised her hands, Joan's eyes fell to the dead body. She couldn't think of Stan as a person. She couldn't picture Carmen as a murderer worthy of being put behind bars. Carmen wasn't a murderer, but she was a killer – on the battlefield and in this motel. And she was about to be arrested for it.

Sam led a pack of four officers as they stormed the room, weapons drawn. He took stock of the scene and saw how much it had deteriorated.

"Carmen, hands behind your head."

The woman carefully raised her hands and interlocked her fingers behind her head. Her eyes were on Joan the entire time as she was patted down, relieved of her gun, and cuffed.

Still pressing Carmen's shirt to her chest, Joan listened to Sam radio for an ambulance. He must have seen the blood. She got to her feet, waving the officer away when he tried to help.

"Can I have your phone?" she asked him, her voice raw from screaming. "I need to call my manager."

Out in the fresh air, Joan watched someone put a hand on Carmen's head to protect her while she got in the back of a police cruiser. Jerry picked up on the last ring. He sounded tired, but he came around when Joan began to explain why he had to do everything in his power to get Carmen out of jail. The manager agreed to meet her at the station, but she told him they would be better off meeting at the hospital since she was probably headed there next.

After returning Sam's phone, the EMTs arrived. Despite the bloody cut on her chest, it was her wrists that hurt the most. Even holding her phone to her ear was excruciating. She'd put herself through the

220

wringer trying to get free during that hellish car ride. Sam accompanied his witness to the hospital. When Jerry showed up, she had just finished getting eight stitches and a brace around her right wrist.

If anyone knew who she was, they didn't say anything. But when she caught her reflection in the mirror of Sam's cruiser, she hardly recognized herself.

At the police station, Joan watched Sam prepare paperwork and wondered if her signature would look awful while her was wrist was out of commission. There were more important things to worry about.

"Carmen's not going to be in trouble, is she?" Joan asked. "She saved my life."

Sam continued to pluck papers from different files in a drawer. "No, this is just procedure. With all the evidence, this case is going to be pretty open and closed. We're going to get her statement and yours, and if I can get her out of jail tonight, I will."

"I know you'll do what you can," Joan whispered. She hoped Carmen wouldn't spend the night at the precinct, but the law was the law. Even if she didn't agree.

Jerry cleared his throat. "Seeing as how we both care about Ms. Savedra's well-being, is there anything I can do to keep this quiet?"

Sam lifted an eyebrow at the manager before pushing a can of pens forward. "Between the First Amendment, the Freedom of Information Act, and public crime reports – you're not keeping this under wraps." He put a clip on the stack of papers before giving them to Joan. "Now, I need to ask you a few questions. Then you'll write out a statement in your own words. And the sooner this gets done, the sooner I can get Carmen out of here. First question is always the hardest. Joan… did you fear for your life tonight?"

Joan didn't want to talk about the event, not right now, maybe not ever, but if it got Carmen out sooner...

"Yes."

Sam nodded as he wrote down her answer. There were a few more basic questions that followed: what time she encountered the perpetrator, if it was the same man who had been shot, and if – in her opinion – everything had been done to try and avoid lethal force.

When that was done, he agreed to let Joan dictate her statement to Jerry, since she was injured and he was sitting right there to watch it happen.

Even though Sam said not to leave anything out, she did decline to mention the reason Carmen left. Joan's forwardness had driven the woman away, and she probably wasn't going to get a second chance.

Sam left to check on Carmen when the paperwork was done. He came back a few minutes later, worry-lines showing on his forehead.

"So? Can you get her out?" Joan asked in a rush.

"She's going to have to stay for the rest of the night. The soonest I can have her out of here is eight in the morning." Sam knew that was a lot less time than most people spent in a cell. It was already past midnight, so maybe Carmen would be one of the lucky ones who could sleep while they were locked up.

Joan's shoulders fell. "Oh." She mulled over things in her head before speaking again. "Can I see her? Just for a few minutes?"

"Let me talk to the captain," Sam said before picking up the phone and dialing a five-digit extension. When the person on the other end answered he talked to them for a few minutes before hanging up again. "Come with me."

222

Joan agreed to meet Jerry at the front desk when she was ready to go and followed Sam through the building. She had expected Carmen to be with the rest of the midnight rabble: drunks and prostitutes, dealers and thieves. But the man didn't lead her past any mass holding cells or down a line of other locked cages. Carmen was sitting on a cot, head in her hands, in a square cell all her own with no one else around.

Approaching quietly, Joan wrapped her one good hand around a vertical metal bar. That was when Carmen finally looked up. Without further prompting, Carmen stood and walked to the edge of her cage. Sam busied himself with inspecting the walls, as respectful of the moment as he could be.

"Hey," Carmen whispered. "How are you doing?"

Joan tried to smile, but she couldn't achieve the feat. "I'm fine, thanks to you." She gripped the post a little tighter and realized that her hand was so cold that the steel felt warm. She would probably be dead if Carmen hadn't shown up when she did. For saving her life, getting thrown into jail wasn't much of a thanks. "Sam said you'll be free to go at eight."

"That's not too long from now."

The rocker nodded. She couldn't think of what else to say. It was her words, her voice that got her into trouble with Stan anyway. Carmen looked just as lost when her eyes swept the floor in quiet thought. The fire they had on the balcony collapsed into a blackened pit of awkward silence.

Where did they go from here?

"Joan... when I get out, I think we should talk."

"Yeah. Whatever you want. I owe you after what you did."

"No, you don't."

Carmen responded so quickly and sincerely that Joan startled. She let go of the bar and furrowed her eyebrows. Of course she owed the bodyguard. What else was there to talk about? This was a business relationship. Maybe, with time and a few coffees, a friendship.

It was Carmen's turn to hang on the bars as she grabbed one with each hand and leaned her forehead against them. She squeezed her eyes shut and huffed.

"Wait. I want to talk now," Carmen said. "Before I lose my nerve." While she had Joan's attention, she straightened up and glanced at her best friend. "Shut your ears, Macrae."

A short, "Yes, Ma'am," went Carmen's way.

With a rattling breath, Carmen inhaled the scent of day-old, harsh cleaners. Everything about this place had her spooked. The slight unevenness of the bars, the disorganized files she saw on her way in, the fact that the light above her was short one working bulb…. Joan was another mess of wild, disordered living. The sink in the penthouse had never been empty every time Carmen visited. Not once, except for the day Carmen stayed and cooked. But what scared her more than a sink full of dishes – more than any time she didn't have control – was eight AM. Real life would resume, and Joan might not be there for her when she got out.

"I could probably take on that list… if you still want me to."

Unfortunately, Joan wasn't quite on the same page. "What?" It had been a long night.

Carmen waved her hand as she blushed. "Your list. Where I'm everything you… you know, *need*."

Joan's postured softened. "Oh, that list." Smiling, she reached out and grabbed one of the bars

224

just below where Carmen was holding. It was the smallest amount of contact between them, but it was enough. "I don't know if I should date someone who's been in jail. What will the public think?"

Carmen chuckled with relief. "They'll think you're the typical rock star, but you're a lot more than that to me."

Before Joan could respond to that, someone made a hushed gagging noise behind them. Carmen scowled at the sergeant, but she would get back at him later. When they were alone.

"Ladies, I hate to interrupt, but it's time to go."

Joan pulled away first, but she didn't get far when Carmen spoke again.

"I know it's a lot to ask, Sam, but do you think you could..." She motioned toward her neck.

With a knowing smile, Sam reached into his pocket and pulled out the clinking metal of Carmen's dog tags. "Don't worry. I wouldn't let them just sit overnight." Dog tags were important to a Marine. It was their life – not something to sit in a pile of stuff, amongst other piles of stuff, even if the owner was in jail.

Carmen met Joan's eyes. "Keep them for me until the morning?"

Joan held out her good hand and swallowed when Sam placed the jewelry around her neck instead. "I'll take good care of them," she promised. She gave Carmen a last look before her eyes watered, and she had to go.

Sam escorted Joan up to the front desk where her manager was waiting for her. "Try and get some rest," he advised. "If you want, you can come back in the morning when Carmen gets released."

Jerry escorted his singer back to her building and told her to take another week off. Joan was

225

thankful for the break. She wouldn't be able to play her guitar until her wrist was healed anyway.

CHAPTER TWENTY-ONE

When 6 AM rolled around that day, Joan didn't know what to do with herself. She couldn't eat, couldn't sleep, and she couldn't wait anymore. She hailed a cab to take her to the police station and arrived an hour and a half early.

Figuring that it was too soon to go inside, Joan sat on the curb outside of the building. The sun was just coming up and tossing light onto the lot of parked police cruisers. She held onto Carmen's dog tags, running her thumb over the letters like it would bring the Marine out sooner.

Instead, time carried on as it always did. Joan envisioned a metronome in her head. The rhythm was persistent, reminding her that there was a backwards tick for every forward pulse. Her first album was supposed to be about balance, or that was the way she portrayed it. But was that true? She got a taste of fame with Despite Darkness and adopted the role of rock diva like it was nothing. She went to all the parties, hit up her under-the-counter pharmacist, and treated some people like garbage. The music was calling her to come back to it.

Around seven, Sam went to the cafeteria to get food for Carmen. An officer stopped him on his way back to the holding area, letting him know about the minor celebrity sitting outside. With food to deliver, he went to the holding cell first.

"Your girl is already here, sitting out front."

"What?" Carmen furrowed her eyebrows.

"Yeah, I heard she's been out there for half an hour already."

"*¡Ay, que ir a por ella, pendejo!*" Carmen said

quickly. Between Maria and Carmen, Sam had picked up a fair amount of Spanish. But he couldn't understand either one of them when they spoke that fast.

"Huh?"

"Go get her, jackass!" Carmen rolled eyes.

He laughed and shook his head, turning to do as he was told. He walked through the station and frowned when he saw a few officers idling and looking out the windows.

"Aren't you supposed to be working, Marco?" The other officer huffed and didn't answer. "What's going on out there?" He stepped toward the front doors and saw that Joan had been accosted by a trio of paparazzi. They always did seem to travel in packs, and they always came around the local stations to find dirt. The ambulance chasers were the worst, but it was like Sam said. The story was going to get out.

"Joan! Ms. Devintia? What happened to your arm?"

"What are you doing here? Joan, look this way, please!"

"Were you arrested last night? What did you do?"

Cameras were closing in. Someone seemed to be recording, but Joan tried not to look at them and kept a hand in front of her face. She didn't want to bail on Carmen, but she couldn't deal with these guys right now.

"Joan," Sam called loudly. "Come inside."

She walked away with the officer, prodding questions still ringing in her ears. There were going to be so many more to come. Even the police officers seemed to be more scrutinizing of her as she stepped inside.

Sam guided her away from the lobby to a conference room with no windows. "You can sit in here. We're going to start processing Carmen out in about ten minutes, so she might be done before eight," he explained. "Do you want some coffee or water while you wait?"

"Coffee, please." She wasn't in it for the caffeine, just the comfort of warmth that she'd been without all night long.

While Joan waited she toyed with Carmen's dog tags again. She had studied them for quite some time, not just reading them but combing the aluminum for nicks and scrapes. She found the jewelry as comforting as Carmen had probably meant it to be. It would be a little difficult to hand them over, but she would do it. So long as she had Carmen, she wouldn't need the embossed artifact.

About forty minutes after Joan had been let inside, Sam brought Carmen into the conference room. Carmen couldn't help but smile, seeing Joan there waiting for her.

"We'll go out the back way," Sam said. He held the door open before taking the lead. Carmen's SUV had already been pulled around, and there wasn't a camera vulture in sight. He told Carmen that she was coming over for dinner tomorrow and that he'd be calling her.

It was quick goodbye, but it was meaningful. And when he was gone, Joan beat Carmen to the passenger door and shook her head.

"Not today, Ms. Savedra."

Carmen folded her arms over her chest. "Ms. Savedra? Joan, what's going on?"

"Jerry wanted me to tell you to call him, but he's just going to tell you that you're fired."

"Fired?"

"With a very large severance check, I promise you." Joan opened the door for herself but waited to step inside. "Oh, and he's going to handle any legal fees that might come up in the future. So, yes. You are fired, and I can open my own doors."

"Hmph." Carmen rocked on her feet. "Maybe I wanted to open the door for a different reason."

"That's sweet," Joan praised with affection. She lifted a hand to the borrowed necklace and took it off. With a gentle reverence, she put the chain back around Carmen's neck. For a second, they both stared at the gleaming tags.

"Joan-"

"Carmen-"

Both women stopped at the same time and laughed.

"You first," the singer relented.

"Would you like to come over for breakfast?"

"I'd love to."

Carmen reached up to tuck her dog tags into her shirt as she grinned wider. "Good. Now, it's your turn. What were you going to say?"

"I was going to ask if I could... kiss you."

The Marine took her time answering as she looked for a good place to rest her hands. "Well, it is on *your* list." Joan's hips would do just fine.

"I have a list?" Joan asked, anticipation making her feel like someone was pounding the pedal on her bass-drum-heart.

Chuckling, Carmen leaned in. "It's a long one, too."

Tucked away from the world, Joan crossed the first thing off her list. It was too late to add songs to *Snowball Earth*, but maybe... maybe the next CD would have a sappy recording or two.

About the Authors

Andrea and Max. They share a home with a cat, Ele Jota Amo Taco Bell Incan Jaguar King (L.J.), and a dog, Earth Wind and Balefire (Bae). They own a combined nineteen Resident Evil movies, impressive, and are unused to talking about themselves in third person.

They are working on a sequel to this story, as well as individual projects. So, hopefully they will get more practice with third person soon.

A Letter from Andrea & Max

Thank you so much for reading our debut novel. It was a dream come true to complete this book. Starting from a world of fanfiction, we have a particular hunger for reviews. Visibility is paramount to our community. We would appreciate it if you took the time to leave a review on Amazon, Goodreads, and any other sites you might be into.

Joan and Carmen aren't finished yet. With your help we hope to make enough money to commission the next cover and hire an editor.

Until next time, friends.

CPSIA information can be obtained
at www.ICGtesting.com
Printed in the USA
BVOW03s2153281117
501513BV00001B/7/P